LIONHEART'S SCRIBE

Karleen Bradford

Lionheart's Scribe

THE THIRD BOOK OF THE CRUSADES

HarperCollins*PublishersLtd*

LIONHEART'S SCRIBE:
THE THIRD BOOK OF THE CRUSADES
Copyright © 1999 by Karleen Bradford.
All rights reserved. No part of this book may be used or reproduced
in any manner whatsoever without prior written permission
except in the case of brief quotations embodied in reviews.
For information address HarperCollins Publishers Ltd,
55 Avenue Road, Suite 2900 Toronto,
Ontario, Canada M5R 3L2.

www.harpercanada.com

HarperCollins books may be purchased for educational, business
or sales promotional use. For information please write:
Special Markets Department, HarperCollins Canada,
55 Avenue Road, Suite 2900 Toronto,
Ontario, Canada M5R 3L2.

First HarperCollins trade paper ed. ISBN 0-00-648116-7
First HarperCollins mass market ed. ISBN 0-00-648511-1

Canadian Cataloguing in Publication Data

Bradford, Karleen
Lionheart's scribe

ISBN 0-00-648511-1

I. Title.

PS8553.R217L56 2000   jC813'.54   C99-930460-7
PZ7.B72Li 2000

OPM 9 8 7 6 5 4
Printed and bound in the United States
Set in Monotype Plantin

To Angie

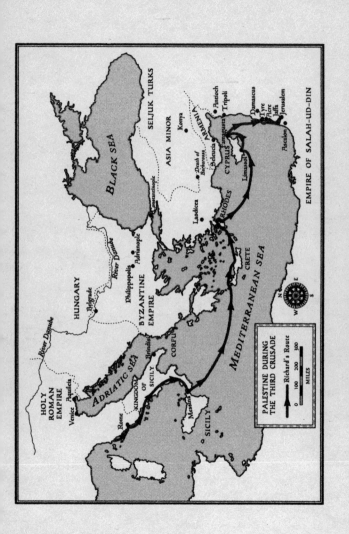

STONE UPON STONE

Stone upon stone a city rises,
Stone upon stone it falls.
Man upon man each war surprises
Altars, buildings, walls.

> David,
> Solomon,
> Nebuchadnezzar,
> Maccabee,
> Herod,
> And Hadrian,
> Constantine,
> Khosrau,
> Saladin,
> And Suleiman.

This is a song we sing to conquerors,
A hymn we make to war,
The straight plumb line of rules and rulers–
That's what fighting's for.

Stone upon stone a city rises,
Stone upon stone it falls.
Man upon man each war surprises
Us all.

From *O Jerusalem* by Jane Yolen

LIONHEART'S SCRIBE

PROLOGUE

† † †

In 1096 Pope Urban II of the Holy Roman Empire called for a crusade to recover Jerusalem from the Muslims and reestablish the pilgrimage paths to the east. A first, abortive People's Crusade, led by a monk called Peter the Hermit, whom many thought mad, set out from Cologne in April of that year. This venture ended in disaster just outside of Constantinople.

The First Crusade, composed of some of the greatest princes and knights in Germany, France and Normandy, set out in August. On July 16, 1099, after three years of hardship and battle, this crusade succeeded in recapturing Jerusalem.

Jerusalem remained Christian for only eighty-eight years, however, before being reconquered by the great Muslim leader Salah-ud-Din, known to many Christians as Saladin. A second crusade failed. The Muslims gradually retook the greater part of Ôutremer—the Christians' empire "over the sea." Led by Salah-ud-Din, they swept up the Mediterranean coast, recapturing most of the important cities, including Acre. King Guy of Jerusalem determined to win back his realm and laid siege to this most important port. In retaliation Salah-ud-Din's army laid siege to the forces of Guy. This stalemate continued for almost two years until a third crusade was organized. Three great kings—Frederick Barbarossa, Emperor of the Holy Roman Empire, King Philip of France and Richard Lionheart of England—joined forces to pledge themselves to the cause. King Frederick set out from Germany, but was drowned on the way. The success of the crusade was left to the two kings, Richard and Philip, who met at Messina on the island of Sicily, in September 1190.

THIS IS THE JOURNAL OF
MATTHEW,
SON OF ROBERT, APPRENTICE
SCRIBE TO VULGRIN OF MESSINA,
ON THE ISLAND OF SICILY

✝   ✝   ✝

The first day of September, the year of our Lord 1190

There was no need to beat me. My master, Vulgrin, is a brute. True, I did ruin several of his best skins, but anyone can spill an inkhorn. It should not have been placed where it was. I'm certain I did not place it there.

And now he has set me to recopying them all. It will take me the whole night!

"It will do you good to practice," he growled at me. "Your hand is almost illegible."

My blood is boiling inside me, fair fit to burst. I must vent my feelings somehow. Vulgrin will never miss this old and torn skin. I will complain on it.

In any case I will be improving my hand, will I not? Serves him right if I steal from him.

The second day of September

It did take me most all of the night. I made my way down to Vulgrin's stall by the harbor this morning in a daze of sleep. So dozed was I that I forgot to be wary. The gang that lies in wait to torment me every morning caught me well and truly by surprise.

"Cripple!" they jeered. "Devil foot! Where's your tail, devil? Show us your tail!" Then they pelted me with filth. It smirched one of the skins I had recopied with so much trouble, and I barely had time to cleanse it before Vulgrin arrived.

All because of my foot. My cursed, crooked foot. Other boys my age have friends—I have naught but enemies. Vulgrin says they taunt me because they are afraid of me. They think that my crippled foot means I have been touched by the devil. Much good that explanation does me. I asked the priest why God should have chosen to punish me this way, and he gave me a cuff on the ear for daring to question His wisdom. That did me no good either.

Truth, it's a miserable life I lead here.

Vulgrin grunted when he saw the work I had done.

"Barely readable," he snarled. "Just barely. I regret the day I promised your father to take you on. You must practice, boy. Work!"

So I stole another old piece of skin and determined to write my side of things again tonight. He wants me to practice? I will practice. But he will provide me with the means. And here I will be able to write the words that *I* choose, not those that someone else tells me to.

The third day of September

It was pouring rain when I awoke this morning. Every single thing in my small hut was sopping wet. The roof needs rethatching, but where am I to get new thatch? Vulgrin pays me with so few coins I can barely buy what I need to eat, and I have nothing to trade. My tunic is full of holes as well, but there is certainly no hope of replacing it.

Why does everything smell so much worse when it is wet? The stench in my hut is like that of a pigsty, and the cobbled streets are slimy with stinking muck. I nearly fell twice before I reached the harbor. The tied-up ships creak and loom and complain in the mist. Everyone is in a foul temper. I had naught to eat but a crust of bread that I had tucked into my tunic. By the time I took it out it was sodden, and the bit of cheese Vulgrin tossed to me was moldy. No one wanted the services of a scribe today either, so Vulgrin was in even more of a temper than usual.

I care not a whit if my hand is improving or not, but I find it a strange kind of relief to scratch out these feelings when I come back to my hut at night. I think I will keep on at it.

The fifth day of September

Vulgrin actually muttered that a list I copied out today for the master of one of the ships was "tolerable." I must be improving.

The tenth day of September

It occurs to me that what I am doing is called keeping a journal. Vulgrin keeps such an account, but it is mostly of the work he does each day and how much he is paid for it. He has headed it up with the words "Daily Journal" and inscribed his name underneath. Each entry is begun with the date of the day he entered it.

I think I will do the same. I will go back and put a date at the beginning of each entry I have made.

More, I will give mine a heading too. "The Journal of Matthew" I will call it. "The Journal of Matthew, son of Robert." And even more, "The Journal of Matthew, son of Robert, apprentice scribe to Vulgrin of Messina, on the island of Sicily."

That has a fine and important ring to it. Cripple I may be, but thanks to my father I can master the writing down of words. That's more than the rabble that hounds me every day can do.

I have run out of skins. I must steal another tomorrow. But I must be certain to keep them well hidden. Vulgrin must not find these scribblings.

The twelfth day of September

The city is in a turmoil. At mass this morning the priests were almost beside themselves with excitement. King Philip of France has arrived. The whole harbor stopped work in order to watch his ships dock. There is a great number of them and they are taking up all of one end. I don't think we have ever seen so many warships here at one time before. From Vulgrin's stall the fleet looked like a forest of masts stretching up to the clouds above.

I was as caught up in the excitement as all the rest and I desperately wanted to see what the king looked like, but Vulgrin cuffed me and put me back to copying out a list of supplies for one of the other ships, so I did not see King Philip come ashore. He has been to pay his respects to our own King Tancred, and I hear he has been lodged in a palace in the city. He is here on crusade—on his way to liberate the Holy City of Jerusalem from the Saracens.

That was a name that was new to me—Saracens. I summoned up the nerve to ask a priest who they were. He said they were Muslims.

"Like the Muslims who live here in Sicily?" I asked.

"The same," he answered.

"But if we live in peace with them here, why can we not do so in Jerusalem?" I said.

"Because Jerusalem belongs to the Christians," he replied.

"Who said so?" I asked.

His face got red and he glared down at me.

"Our Lord God, of course," he answered. "You would know that if you'd been attending to the sermons."

I probably should have stopped there, but I couldn't. Perhaps the same devil that gave me my crooked foot gave me this irresistible urge to ask questions.

"Who did God say it to?"

Now I have to do penance for the rest of the day, and if I ever ask him another question he will see to it that Vulgrin drives me out of the city and I'll never be allowed to return.

The thirteenth day of September

There is talk of naught but the crusade everywhere in the city. It is to be a grand and holy war. How wonderful it would be to be a part of it. I am careful to keep my mouth shut and not ask questions, but I am listening to everything. This is the most exciting thing that has happened on this island for as long as I can remember.

Another king is coming to join King Philip, they say—King Richard of England, the one they call Lionheart because he is so brave in battle. The two kings will meet here and then sail together to the Holy Land. I will find a way to see him, Vulgrin or no Vulgrin. My mother was English and I learned the English language from her. She used to sing to me, and recite long stories that sounded so sweet, they put me to sleep. I do not remember her well, but I remember her voice and those beautiful words.

Vulgrin thinks my enthusiasm for the English king is stupid. He says Richard is a Norman, like my father was. I asked him how, therefore, Richard could be king of England? He boxed my ears and told me not to ask foolish questions. I suppose I will never learn. But I think perhaps he does not know the answer himself.

The fourteenth day of September

Vulgrin has been especially horrible to me lately. I take great pleasure in stealing skins from him and writing words about him that he will never see. It gives me a power I've never had before.

The fifteenth day of September

I roused myself early this morning and was down at the harbor before dawn. The Muslim call to prayer was just dying away and the first rays of the sun were beginning to show against the dark night sky. It was so quiet. I have never been down there at that time before. Usually there is such a horde of people and such noise and confusion that it makes my head spin. The fishmongers had not yet arrived and there was a fresh, salty smell to the air. I sat on a log near the water and looked at the king of France's war galleys. They are such great ships!

Looking at those vessels, I began to feel a very strange sensation inside me. What would it be like to sail on one of them? To go as far as I can see from here, and then go yet farther, on to new and distant lands?

It was very odd. The feeling inside me became so strong it actually hurt.

Men started moving around within the ships, fires were lit and curses rang out. I stirred myself and had Vulgrin's stall set up with all the writing materials out and ready by the time he arrived. You would think he might have been a little grateful, but no, he just grumbled and pushed me aside.

There was a lot of work to do today. We tallied lists of stores for the masters of the ships and wrote letters without stop. Vulgrin might complain about my writing, but at least I have a good knowledge of languages. My father taught me well. I can speak even more languages than I can write. It seems I have a talent that way. People congregate in Messina from all over, and more tongues are spoken here than anywhere else in the world, I warrant. I hear the words and I can learn the meaning of them almost without trying, it seems.

I consider it a talent. Vulgrin considers anything he cannot do himself a waste of time. Still, on the rare occasion when someone wants something written in English, it is I who must do it. Not that he will admit as much, of course. He just nods at me as if the matter were of too little importance for him to deal with, and says, "The boy will do it."

My father was a far greater scribe than Vulgrin was. Vulgrin may not think I remember, but I do. My father spent hours with me. He taught me how to write the words and my mother taught me how to make them have a life of their own. And I too will be a better scribe than Vulgrin one day. I *will*!

What a lot I have written tonight. I shall have to steal more skins, but I had better be careful. Vulgrin was counting them today with a frown on his face, even the old and torn ones. I must write as small as I can and get as much as possible on each scrap.

The twentieth day of September

According to the gossip I hear at the harbor, the priests are preaching crusade from every church. They are urging everyone who is fit to take up the cross and join. A fever seems to have taken hold of the city. It has even infected me. I watched the crusading knights at mass this morning. They are so magnificent. Their crosses burn on their breasts with the glory of God. If only I were strong and able-bodied, I would be one of the first to volunteer to join them. What a marvelous thing it would be to march to Jerusalem, to fight God's Holy War! But who would want me, cripple that I am? I would be useless.

The twenty-first day of September

One of the crusaders stopped by our stall today. He wanted a letter written to his lady wife back in the Frankish lands. Of course, Vulgrin would not let me write it, but I stayed within earshot as the knight dictated it. In his letter the knight promised his lady that they would sail to the Holy Land, reconquer Jerusalem and be home by Yuletide. He sounded so proud and confident.

I heard Vulgrin give a snort as he was writing, and when he had finished I summoned up the nerve— or the idiocy—to ask him why. For once he didn't chastise me.

"They're fools. All of them. Jerusalem was conquered by the Saracens almost a hundred years ago. If retaking the city were so easy, someone would have done so long ago," he growled.

I decided to press my luck. "Has anyone tried?" I asked.

"They haven't stopped trying, you ninny. And nobody's been able to do it," he replied.

I was shocked to hear him speak so. No one else in the city does. It must be that he is old and angry and bitter about everything. Sometimes I know how that feels. Not about being old, I mean, but certainly about being angry and bitter.

I look at those great ships and see King Philip's huge army camped out on the fields outside the walls of the city. How could the crusade not be successful? And there is still Richard Lionheart of England to come with his army as well.

Of course they will be victorious.

The twenty-second day of September

He arrived today: Richard, king of England. I knew immediately when I saw him why men call him Lionheart. He is as glorious as the sun itself. I don't think I have ever felt such a stirring within me as I did when I first laid eyes on him. Vulgrin can snort all he wants, but this is a king worthy of the name.

My quill is dashing ahead too quickly. I will collect myself and record everything as it happened. This has been such a day. I must write down every single detail of it. This journal will be something to read and relive when the crusaders have all gone and I have returned to my usual boring life.

When I awoke this morning the rumors were already knifing around the town.

"A fleet is sailing toward our harbor!" I heard a man cry.

"An immense fleet!" shouted another. "The sky is billowing with sails!"

I was up and out of my hut in a trice. I knew it must be the king of England.

I hobbled as quickly as I could down to the harbor. It seemed as if the whole town was on its way there too. I was jostled and bumped and almost trodden upon. My foot began to pain me even more than usual, and I cursed it with each step for slowing me down. Twice, slipping in the filth that ran beneath my feet, I fell, but that only made me hurry more. I was afraid there would be such a crowd lining the shore by the time I got there that I wouldn't see a thing.

I needn't have worried. King Richard did not sail quietly in the way King Philip did.

As I feared, a swarm of people already lined the harborside when I finally got there. But because I am small for my fifteen years and agile, despite my foot, I slipped between them like an eel and forced my way through to the very front. Being spindle-shanked has its advantages. My elbows are sharp and bony enough to jab most effectively at ribs and fat bellies.

And what a sight I saw. On the horizon was a fleet of ships, so many that when I tried to count them, I had to give up. Sails filled the entrance to our harbor. Then I heard from over the water the shrill bugling of trumpets. The sound sent a shiver down my spine. I don't know when I have ever been so excited. I stood planted to the spot and didn't give way to anybody, no matter how hard they pushed.

As the fleet came nearer I could see that most of the vessels were warships painted in every possible color. Even their sails were brilliantly hued and shone against the blue sky. The railings of the ships seemed to be ringed with glittering fire. At first I couldn't imagine what was aflame, but then I realized that the crusaders had hung their shields all around and they were reflecting back the sun.

The sea boiled as the oarsmen drove the ships on. Then I saw what I had come to see.

The leading ship was a galley painted a crimson as red as blood. It flew King Richard's pennant, three golden lions on a scarlet background. In the prow stood the king himself. He wore a cloak of gold that streamed back from his shoulders in the wind and his hair was just as golden. He seemed to be standing on a raised platform—perhaps so that everyone could see him? His legs were planted wide apart and he stood firmly, confident and steady in spite of the tossing deck beneath his feet.

I drank in the sight. Never have I seen anything more splendid. This is how a king should look. In that moment I felt such a longing surge up in me. It was stronger even than the strange feeling I had the other night when I sat by the harbor and watched the king of France's ships rocking at their moorings. Perhaps it is all the talk of crusade, perhaps it is the sight and smell of these foreign ships, but I long to be on one of them. To be one of the men I see here every day who are going to sail far away to new countries, new adventures. To do my part to regain Jerusalem. To do God's will.

But what nonsense I am writing. It is impossible and I know it.

The twenty-third day of September

I could not write anymore last night. My fingers were cramped and my quill too dull. I have sharpened it today though, and I must continue. I know full well that I will never see such a sight again and I do not want to forget any of it.

Forty-six oars drove King Richard's warship on. I counted. It sailed smoothly into the harbor. As it approached the pier, the great square sail suddenly went limp. One last sweep of the ship's oars brought the great vessel alongside, and then the oars were raised skyward, all together. A command rang out and they lapped down, one by one, to lie in rows along the inside of the ship. It was so neatly done. During the whole time King Richard stood with his cloak billowing around him.

A great cheer went up from every person on the shore.

"He has a great enthusiasm for war, does England's Richard," I heard a man behind me say. I can well imagine that to be true.

As soon as his ship was tied up the king leaped ashore without waiting for assistance of any kind. That seemed to upset the nobles and the other important men standing there waiting to receive him. They probably had a whole ceremony planned, but this king is obviously a man who does things his own way. Trumpets and clarions sounded, a little raggedly, as if they had been taken by surprise. Then King Philip strode forward out of the crowd. The two kings embraced and I was finally able to get a look at the king of France. He is as tall as King Richard, but I thought he had a sly look about him. I would not trust him if I were the king of England.

More cheers rang out. I found I was cheering as loudly as everyone else. I shouted until my voice turned hoarse. In my fervor I threw my cap in the air. That was a mistake, for when it came down, some other hands grabbed it and I never saw it again. It was my only head covering and my ears will suffer for it when the weather turns cold.

I made my way back to Vulgrin's stall, but couldn't keep my mind on my work. I made stupid mistakes and blotted two skins. I think Vulgrin tired himself out beating me. But I could not think of anything other than the sight of Richard Lionheart, king of England, sailing into our harbor.

The thirtieth day of September

I thought that King Richard would lodge in a palace in the city, as does King Philip of France, but instead he has settled his army outside the city walls. It is a huge encampment. They say he has five thousand men with him.

I could not wait to finish my work with Vulgrin today so that I could go to see for myself. In my haste I ruined another skin and received another good beating for it. In a way that was a blessing though, as Vulgrin was beside himself with anger. He stormed away after he had beaten me and shouted for me to get out of his sight, so I was able to get away early. I managed to steal the skin I ruined too. Now that I have so many interesting things to write about, I do not intend to stop.

I stuffed the skin down the front of my tunic and made my way to one of the city gates where I could look down on the camp. There are pavilions and tents spread out as far as a man can see. Soldiers mill around everywhere. On the fields beyond the camp I saw a troop of knights mounted on enormous horses charging at each other with spears lowered. I suppose they were only practicing, but it looked like a real battle to me and I caught my breath as they knocked each other off their horses at a great rate.

On top of one big pavilion, off to the far side, flew

a royal streamer with three golden lions roaring on it. I realized that had to be the tent of King Richard himself. I watched it for as long as I could, hoping I might catch a glimpse of the king, but to no avail. Then a city guard came and chased me away.

I'm going to go back though. As soon as I can.

The second day of October

King Philip tried to sail today, but the weather was foul. The storms and the wind were too much for him, and after but a few hours his ships came limping back, sails hanging torn and bedraggled. I was there to watch as they straggled into the harbor. I heard one man laugh when he saw them.

"The king of France gets seasick," he said. "I imagine he's puking his innards out right now."

Not very heroic, that. I'll wager the king of England doesn't get seasick.

The third day of October

The talk amongst the crusaders who frequent the quayside is that the armies in the Holy Land have been hemmed in at Acre by Salah-ud-Din, the Muslim leader whom many Christians call Saladin. They are desperate for the arrival of King Richard and King Philip, I hear, and the crusaders are desperate to go, but winter is almost upon us and it seems now they might have to wait for spring. It is probably unchristian of me to say so, but I hope they do. I want to see more of them. I do not want them to leave.

The fifth day of October

I got into the camp today! And by a very clever ruse. There is a persistent nanny goat that noses around my hut constantly and has been no end of a nuisance to me. She seems to have no owner and is determined to eat what little roof I have left. Early this morning I was awakened by a tremendous commotion over my head and a cloud of dirt and dust falling upon me. I knew it must be the goat. There are a few leaves still on some of the branches that I have patched the holes with, and she has had her eye on them. At first I just lay there and cursed at her. Then I had an idea.

I leaped out of bed and dashed outside, just as she jumped down and tried to escape. I was too quick for her, however. I grabbed her horns and tied her to a spindly tree in front of my hut. She objected mightily, but when I found a handful of straw for her to munch on, she settled down. Then, just at the break of day, I led her out of the city.

"Where are you going, brat?" the guard at the gate demanded when he saw me.

"I have been commissioned to supply someone in the camp with a good milking goat," I answered as boldly as I could.

"There are goats all over this cursed island," he said. "Why would anyone want another one?"

Truth, it was a good question and for a moment I was at a loss for words, so I just stood there and looked foolish. Sometimes that is not difficult. The guard glowered at me, but when I still could not come up with an answer, he muttered something about the stupidity of foreigners and the dim-wittedness of boys and waved me through.

As I drew near to the camp I was almost over-come by the noise and by the smells. The city is bad enough, of course, and I am used to it, but this place was worse. Men shouted, women yelled, children screamed. This is an army that travels with a multitude of pilgrims as well as knights and soldiers, and it makes for a mighty disorder. I saw food cooking, but any good smells from the pots were over-powered by the stink of the trenches dug around the camp to serve as latrines. They were already over-flowing. A dog snapped at the heels of my little goat and she skittered nervously. I began to wonder just what I was going to do with her. I had used her as an excuse to get into the camp, but I hadn't the vaguest notion of what to do with her now.

Just then a woman called out to me.

"Is that a good milking goat?" she bellowed.

"Oh, yes," I answered straightaway. Not that I had the slightest idea of whether she was or not, as I have no taste for milk and had never tried to milk her, but it seemed a sensible thing to say.

"I need milk for my little ones. There are goats all around here, but I cannot for the life of me catch one, they are so quick and shy. Will you give me the loan of her for an hour or so? I can offer you some bread and cheese in exchange," she added.

My stomach growled and decided the issue for me.

"That I will," I replied. I handed over the rope to her. She, in return, gave me a knob of fresh bread and a chunk of soft new cheese. I left, wolfing the food down in such big bites that I almost choked. I have not eaten so well in months.

I prayed the nanny would cooperate.

Then I set to exploring the camp. I drew as near as I dared to the pavilion of King Richard, but his guards chased me away. I did, however, find the stables where they are keeping the horses. I have always liked horses, but I have never seen any such as these. Compared to our wiry little island ponies these beasts are immense. Their backs are higher than my head, their limbs are like tree trunks and their hooves are bigger than the flat loaves of bread the baker makes. They are all shades, from black, to gray, to dun colored. They have long, tangled manes and tails, and their heads are big and wide.

I slipped in and wandered around amongst them. They did not mind my presence. Some even welcomed me with soft snuffling noises. Horses, it seems, do not fear a crippled boy. The smell of horse hung over everything. I like that smell. It is sharp and pungent and warm.

Then one of the guards saw me. I prepared to run, but he stopped me.

"You, boy," he called. "Fill those buckets with grain and be quick about it."

I suppose he thought I was a stable boy. What a piece of luck! I ran to do his bidding.

"Go on, then," he growled when I had filled the buckets. "Get on with feeding the beasts."

I must confess I was more than a little nervous when I approached the first horse. It did look big. I held the bucket out, ready to flee at the slightest sign of danger. To my surprise and great relief, the animal just swung its heavy head around and stared at me with huge, dark eyes, as if sizing me up, then calmly settled in to eating.

The sun was rising by then and I realized I was going to be late getting to my work with Vulgrin. When the guard's back was turned I slipped out. I hope the real stable boy turned up to carry on with the feeding. I wouldn't like to think of the horses going hungry. Still, I imagine valuable animals like that would not be neglected. Truth, they probably eat better than I do.

I made my way quickly back to the tent where I had left the goat. I hid behind a tree when I got there and watched for a few moments, trying to see if the nanny had been a success or whether it would be wiser not to show my face. The woman was boiling up some sort of stew on the fire and the goat was tied to a bush nearby, munching on the sparse grass. Two infants tumbled around the woman's feet. They were enormously dirty, but seemed content enough, so I made my way forward.

"How was my goat?" I asked as the woman looked up. "Did she satisfy you?"

"She's a marvelous goat," she answered. "She gave as much milk as we needed and more besides. Can you bring her each morning?"

"That I most certainly can," I answered, delighted that I now had the means of getting into the camp every day. "I will bring her here for milking every day. In return for bread and cheese," I added quickly. I thought I might as well make the best bargain I could while I was at it.

"So you liked my cheese," she said. She smiled so hugely that her wide, red face seemed almost to crack in half. "Make it myself, I do."

"I liked it indeed," I answered. "It was the best cheese I have ever tasted." That was no lie, but I did not see fit to tell her that most of the cheese I ate was sour and moldy.

"Well, as long as your little nanny supplies me with milk, I'll give you all the cheese you want," she said, fair bursting with pride.

"Done," I said.

I think I have the best of that deal, especially since the goat isn't even mine in the first place.

I untied the nanny and led her out of the camp, very pleased with myself and with her. She seemed like a fine little beast to me now. I even tried to pat her on the head, but she bit me.

"See you tomorrow," I called cheerily to the guard at the gate as I passed back in.

He shook his head and made another remark about the idiocy of foreigners, but he knows now that I will be passing back and forth and he will not bother me again, I am sure. I will have to go early though, so as not to be late for my work with Vulgrin. Even if I am, I do not care. I want to find out as much as I can about this camp and these crusaders. Perhaps I can feed the horses every day. I like horses. I would like to do that.

I shut the goat in my hut for safety—she is just contrary enough to decide to wander off and desert

me now that I have found a use for her—and made
my way to the docks to Vulgrin. He gave me a
wallop because I was late, but I hardly noticed it.

The seventh day of October

There have been interesting rumors going around
the city. Working with Vulgrin down at the harbor
has one excellent advantage: I hear all the news.

The arrival of all these armies from the north seems
to have unsettled everybody on the island. The
crusaders can't seem to understand how we all get
along together here—the Arabs with the Greeks, the
Normans with the Italians, the Muslims with the
Christians. They make no effort to get along with us,
I must admit (but only to this journal). Their high-
handed ways make the townspeople furious and
Vulgrin angriest of all, in spite of the increased work
they bring him. I would not give him the satisfaction
of agreeing with him about anything though, so I
keep my mouth closed. The soldiers seem to have a
special dislike for the Greeks amongst us, and the
Greeks call them "long-tailed English devils." To
make matters worse King Richard is angry with our
King Tancred.

Vulgrin has a friend who likes to sit and gossip
with him and I, of course, listen as hard as I can even
while I'm pretending not to, and I get all the news
that way. According to this fellow King Tancred's
father, old King William, was married to King
Richard's sister, Joanna. When the old king died,
King Tancred imprisoned Queen Joanna in one of
his castles and took all her dowry for himself.

"A fortune in gold and jewels," he said, and I could see his eyes grow big at the thought of it. "But even more important than the dowry to King Richard," he went on, "is the fact that the old king had promised him many good, sturdy galleys for the crusade, and King Tancred is keeping those to himself as well."

Out of the corner of my eye I could see Vulgrin staring avidly at the man, picturing all that treasure, I vow. Neither of them seemed too concerned about the fate of Queen Joanna. I should think King Richard is though. I doubt even the galleys could be more important to him than his own sister.

At that point Vulgrin looked over at me and caught me staring.

"Get on with your work, boy," he snapped. "These are not matters that concern you."

But he is wrong. Everything to do with the crusade concerns me. It is all that fills my mind these days.

The twentieth day of October

The mood in King Richard's camp is getting more and more ugly. When I led my little goat in this morning, one of the soldiers spat at me.

"Get out of here, Greek!" he yelled.

"I'm not Greek, I'm English!" I shouted back. It seemed prudent to adopt my mother's nationality today. Still, I made certain to avoid him on my way back.

The first day of November

I am still shaking as I write this. If I ever made as many blots and splotches on a skin that I was writing for Vulgrin as I already have on this one, he would throw me in the sea with a stone around my neck, I'm sure.

I woke yesterday to screams and shouts. People were running back and forth through the streets crying that the long-tailed English devils were coming to murder us all in our beds. I was simple-minded enough to think all the fuss nothing more than a good excuse for not going to work with Vulgrin. I secured my goat and set forth like the greatest of idiots to find out what was going on. Much better had I stayed in my hut and never poked my nose out.

What was going on was that King Richard had finally lost patience. He had attacked the city! At first I could see nothing but our own townspeople milling around, bleating like sheep, then King Tancred's forces stormed down the street where I was making my way. I just managed to shrink back into a doorway as they charged by. They were truly frightening. I have often seen them training, but this was different. They looked half crazed and were screaming war cries as they ran. This was not practice—this was real!

From where I hid I could see the main gate of the city. It was this gate that King Richard and his men were attacking. Even as I watched it gave way with a huge, splintering crash. I saw the king himself drive through at the head of his men, swinging an axe around his head and shouting just as loudly as any of them. I froze and forgot to breathe.

The two armies met with a roar. I covered my ears and flattened myself back even farther into my nook as spears thudded onto shields, and swords clanged and clashed all around me. My ears rang with the noise—they are ringing still. Then, added to all the terror, I could hear men screaming as the spears thrust home into flesh. There was so much blood! It was like a scene from hell.

The fighting surged toward me, then past, as King Richard's forces fought their way into the city. I have never been so frightened in my life. I would never admit this to anyone, but I will write it down here—when I thought one of the soldiers had seen me and was coming straight toward my hiding place I pissed myself in my panic. He raced by me, however, and I cowered there until the noise of the battle faded into the distant streets.

I will continue writing tomorrow. I cannot think more on it tonight.

The third day of November

It has been a great victory for King Richard. He vanquished our king thoroughly. King Tancred has given in to his every demand, so the gossip goes, and has released Queen Joanna into the English king's care.

"It would have taken longer for a priest to say Matins than it took the king of England to capture Messina," I heard an old man say.

I am having trouble making sense of all that has

happened, but I will continue writing from where I left off the other night. It is all I can do, and it might help me to sort through my confused thoughts.

It took me more than two hours to reach the safety of my hut. I was forced to duck and hide whenever I saw soldiers approaching. They were hewing and hacking at any person who got in their way, and torching houses. I was worried that my hut would be destroyed, but it was intact. The goat was bleating with fright and had wound her tether ten times around her neck and half-strangled herself, but no soldiers had found this back alley. I boarded up the door and quaked inside, clutching the goat to me for comfort.

It didn't end there.

All the next day and on into the night, King Richard's soldiers plundered and looted, completely out of control. Their commanders made no effort at all to stop them.

I suppose I should feel sympathy for the townspeople and anger at the English king for what he has done to them. I suppose I should feel that these are my people who have been harmed. I do not though. No one on this island has shown me the least bit of kindness in my whole life since my mother and father died. The guards in King Richard's stables treat me better than anyone here ever has. And King Richard had just cause. How could he not have acted to free his own sister?

But I cannot forget the monstrosity of it. Is this the reward that soldiers take in return for risking their lives? Is this the only way they can work off the bloodlust of battle? Perhaps it is fortunate that I am a cripple. I could never be a soldier. Perhaps that is just cowardice, but that is the way of it.

The eleventh day of November

Life in Messina has still not settled down to normal. I wonder if it ever will.

The thirtieth day of November

There is an uneasy kind of peace now. The townsfolk still cast nervous glances over their shoulders, but they are beginning to go about their business again. I am back working down at the harbor with Vulgrin. No one taunts the foreign soldiers anymore though, and people hasten to get out of their way whenever they appear. Vulgrin fawns in a most disgusting way over any of them who come to him to write letters. The two kings, however, now seem to be on the best of terms, at least in public. It is most odd. They are preparing for the Yuletide festivities and the priests are preaching the holiness of the crusade with even more fervor.

"It is God's will," my priest says. He paints the most wondrous pictures of Jerusalem and of the Church of the Holy Sepulcher, which is one of the most holy places in Christendom. He talks of the divine joy of walking the streets where Our Lord Jesus trod. When I listen to him my mind fills with glorious visions. I forget the horror of what happened here. I want nothing more than to be a part of it all.

What will it be like to watch the crusaders sail

away? To remain behind, with nothing to do for the rest of my life but toil away as a slave to Vulgrin?

The first day of December

I have started going back into the camp, and the spirits there are so high after their great victory that no one bothers me. All is preparation for feasts and celebrations. King Richard is a great lover of music and poetry, I have heard, and is even a poet himself. How strange that seems for a man of war such as he is. But it is true. A few times I have managed to creep close enough to his pavilion to hear the sound of minstrels playing and once I heard a lady laughing. I wonder if it was the Queen Joanna. They say she is a great beauty and a kindly lady.

King Philip keeps to himself. No one seems to have a good word to say for him. The talk is that he despises music and all kinds of learning. Considers them a waste of time for a man. He is jealous too of King Richard's victory.

The second day of December

I am back to working regularly at the stables and being beaten regularly by Vulgrin for arriving late in the mornings.

The fifth day of December

There is such a bustle in the camp getting ready for the Yuletide festivities. The excitement has spilled over into the city too and seems to be helping people forget what happened. Only the Christians are involved, of course, not the Muslims.

Mistress Matilde, the woman who rents my goat, is making cheeses at such a great rate that she doesn't even have time to talk. She lets her children run wild and keeps the youngest tethered on a long rope to a tree so that she doesn't have to keep running after it. It is a boy, I think, but so dirty and ragged that it is hard to know for certain.

King Richard is building a wooden castle outside the city, and it is said he will celebrate the festivities there. The framework already looms over the walls. I imagine King Tancred is not too happy with that, especially since the English soldiers boast that the name of the castle is Mategriffon, which means Greek killer.

There is plenty of fuel for the gossips down at the docks these days. Now it seems that King Richard and King Philip are at outs with each other. Vulgrin's friend, whose name is Audebert, but whom I secretly call Mouseface because that's what he looks like, says that King Richard was betrothed to King Philip's sister, the Princess Alice, but now refuses to marry her. There was a scandal involving the princess, who lived at the English court for many years, and King Richard's own father, King Henry!

These great people do like to make trouble for themselves.

The second day of January in the new year of our Lord 1191

What a Yuletide celebration! I left my goat with Mistress Matilde, abandoned Vulgrin completely and spent the whole time in the camp. The soldiers

in the stables have adopted me as a kind of pet, and
they let me sleep there during the festivities. I work
as hard as I can for them and now tend the horses
as confidently as they. The horses recognize me and
each one greets me as I bring it food or curry its
mane and tail. Indeed, it seems the animals are
quieter and more at ease when I am around, and the
soldiers realize this. They are happy to have me do
the work and I am content to be so accepted. It
makes for a much more interesting life than I have
led up to now.

I have never feasted so well in my life. For the
first time I had as much as I could eat every day and
as much wine as I wanted. Of course, I gorged
myself until I was sick and the wine, which I am not
accustomed to, made my head swim and then ache,
but it was worth it.

The first day of February

I have been so busy going back and forth between
the crusaders' camp and Vulgrin's stall that I have
not had time to write in this journal. Nor have I had
skins. Vulgrin was so furious with me for deserting
him over Yuletide that he has been at me constantly
and I had no chance to steal any until today. My
back is raw from the beatings I have taken, and my
ears ring like church bells from being boxed so often.

This is no kind of life. I wish with all my heart
that I could escape from it. But how? Where
could I possibly go? This is an island. I would
have to stow away on a ship, but I would most
certainly be discovered and thrown overboard if I

did that. The only solace I get is from stealing off to King Richard's camp, no matter how many beatings I get for it. But when they leave I will not have even that.

The fifteenth day of February

The soldiers in King Richard's camp are getting impatient and the French even more so. The two kings have kept their armies busy building siege machines, and preparing for the voyage and the siege to liberate Acre that will come after it, but this is not what these men left home for. They talk freely now in front of me, and in spite of the gifts that King Richard has distributed among them to appease them they are angry. They want to get on with the crusade. The seas are not favorable yet, however. There are still too many winter storms. The waves yesterday were so high, they were breaking on the shore right up to the doorsteps of the merchants' houses.

Even though ships are not entering the harbor either, Vulgrin is never without work for me to do. I am finding it harder and harder to sneak away to the crusaders' camp.

The second day of March

King Richard still will not marry King Philip's sister, Alice, and the two kings will not even speak to each other.

This news courtesy of Mouseface.

The fourth day of March

Tempers are running so high in this city that the streets are awash with men fighting and women screaming at them and at each other. I've seen two bodies floating in the harbor. The English soldiers fight with the French, and they all fight with everybody else in the city, whether they be Arab, Norman or Sicilian. An English soldier had an argument with a local woman baker yesterday and before anyone knew what was happening a riot broke out. I ran into it on my way home. Two men set upon me with clubs, but then they started arguing between themselves and while they were at it I escaped as fast as I could hobble.

There are too many people squeezed onto this small island!

The first day of April

King Philip has set sail! His ships were disappearing over the horizon as I made my way down to Vulgrin's stall this morning. I stood and watched them until I couldn't see them anymore. I felt such envy of the men sailing on them that I didn't even notice when Vulgrin greeted me with a harder than usual box on the ear.

Mouseface reported that King Richard is also making his preparations to leave, but is waiting for his mother, Queen Eleanor of Aquitaine, to arrive. She is not to go on the crusade, but he must wait for her nonetheless. Mouseface raised his eyebrows and hooded his eyes and looked down his nose wisely when he told us this, as if to let us know that *he* knew the reason the king had to wait, but I do not believe he does.

I did manage to find out why Richard, a Norman, is king of England though. It seems that he was born in Aquitaine, his mother's land, but his father was King Henry II of England and he was a Norman. King Henry's great grandfather was William of Normandy, whom they call the Conqueror—because he conquered England, of course, and became its king. And that's why a Norman sits on the throne of England.

Mouseface informed me with great authority that King Richard preferred to spend his time in Aquitaine, where the court is famous for its troubadours and poets. He only went to England barely long enough to be crowned king after his father died. The king makes little secret of the fact that he detests the place and cannot speak English at all. I wonder what my mother would have thought of that.

The second day of April

Queen Eleanor arrived, and now we know why King Richard had to wait for her. She brought with her Princess Berengaria of Spain, and King Richard is to wed her instead of Princess Alice! Queen Eleanor and King Richard must have had it planned that she should arrive after King Philip had left. The king of France will have a fit of apoplexy when he finds this matter out. Princess Berengaria is to sail on the same ship as Queen Joanna. She and the king cannot marry before they go because it is Holy Week.

What a tangle these people make of their lives.

The seventh day of April

At mass this morning I listened to the priest blessing the crusade and I watched the crusaders kneeling there, so proud with their red crosses gleaming
on their breasts and shoulders, and I could hardly
sit still. I prayed to God to let me change this life of
mine somehow. Was that a sin? I suppose I should
accept the lot God has given me without question.
That is what my priest says. It is the life hereafter
that matters, not this one.

The tenth day of April

Sebrand, the soldier who is most friendly to me,
told me not to come back again. They are leaving
tomorrow. I am almost desperate with grief. I knew
this day would come, but now that it has, how can
I bear it?

The eleventh day of April

What a difference in my life one day has made. I
read my last sentence, written only yesterday, and I
cannot believe it. My whole world has changed in
just that short space of time.

I am on one of the crusaders' ships—on Queen
Joanna's own ship, in fact. And I am going on
crusade!

This is how it came to pass. I must write it all
down even if it takes me all night—it is such a miracle. Surely God *was* listening to my prayers at mass
the other day.

I was down at the docks with the sunrise this
morning, determined to see the English fleet sail off.

Vulgrin had not yet arrived, so I set up the stall and put out all the writing materials. Then I watched.

The harbor was in turmoil. I could see nothing of the king and the rest of the nobility. I supposed they were already on board their ships. The soldiers and common men were loading the ships amidst a flurry of curses and shouts. I could see crates and barrels of foodstuffs being manhandled onto the decks and lashed down, as well as a huge assortment of other goods. There looked to be supplies of just about everything a ship could need. I am so used to writing down lists that I began to make a list in my head of all that was being loaded onto the ships. There were rudders, anchors, canvas for sails, oars and ropes of every kind. I stared as long-handled iron-tipped lances were carried on, as well as shields, bows, crossbows, quivers of arrows and all the other equipment necessary for knights and soldiers. I wondered how the ships could hold so many things.

There was a smell of tar in the air that mingled with the salt of the sea. I sniffed it up in huge draughts. Gulls swooped and dove for the harbor garbage, screaming and fighting. The sea sparkled and beckoned. The wind blew through my hair and seemed to tease me.

"Come to sea," it seemed to whisper. "Come to sea."

Oh, how I wished I could!

As I was watching they brought up the horses. The soldiers led the massive beasts down to the shore where planks spanned the gap between ship and dock. I saw Sebrand lead King Richard's own stallion up to the plank. That one is my favorite horse of all. I have grown fond of it and I swear it is fond of me.

At the edge of the plank the stallion balked. Sebrand tugged at the bridle. The stallion tossed its head and I could see its eyes roll. Again Sebrand urged the horse forward, but then the beast reared. Its enormous hooves flashed against the sky and Sebrand ducked back just in time to avoid them. Then the rest of the horses lining up behind the stallion began to get nervous. As I watched they began to dance around and one or two of them reared up as well. In an instant a kind of madness spread amongst them.

Without thinking I ran forward. I grabbed the stallion's bridle, which was flying loose, and began to talk to the horse in the voice that I used in the stables. I had to dodge a flying hoof myself, but then the stallion seemed to recognize me. It calmed, and shuddered when I stroked its withers. Urging it on with gentle little noises I headed toward the gangplank. The horse followed me. As it put one hoof on the wooden plank it threw its head back and would have balked again, but I kept up my stream of comforting nonsense.

"Come on, boy. Don't be frightened," I crooned. "Follow me, boy. Come on . . . "

I must admit I was hugely relieved when the animal took one step, then another, after me. I had acted without thinking about the consequences, only sure in my own mind that I could get the horse to do my bidding. Nevertheless, to be truthful, I was as surprised as the others when I actually managed to lead it on board.

From then on it was easy. I led each horse onto the ship. They followed me like puppy dogs. The soldiers were most impressed, and I did my best not to limp. There were forty warhorses and two delicate palfreys that belong to Queen Joanna and the Princess Berengaria. That was how I found out that this is the ship they sail on.

When all the horses were loaded down in the bowels of the galley, I went from one to the other, reassuring them, seeing that they were well tethered and feeding them handfuls of grain. The motion of the ship, even though it was still moored, confused me at first. I stumbled a few times, but luckily no one seemed to notice. By the time Sebrand came to check on the horses I had accommodated myself and was walking fairly steadily.

They finished loading the ship. Shouts and commands from above decks and on shore told me they were about to cast off. Sebrand opened his mouth to speak and I knew he was going to order me ashore.

Suddenly, I knew I could not let them go without me.

"Let me stay," I cried. The words burst out of me.

Sebrand frowned. I was just as surprised as he. I had had no intention at all of saying such a thing, but I couldn't stop myself. "You saw how I managed the horses," I begged. "You see how I can care for them. Please. Let me go with you!" I stared at him and put all my heart into my eyes. I think I even stopped breathing.

He was silent for a long moment. Then, miraculously, he laughed.

"Well, why not?" he roared. "You're so small, we won't have to feed you much, and you are useful . . ." He frowned again. "You'll have to stay down here with the horses though," he said. "Mind, I don't want to see you above decks while we're at sea. You'd get in the way for a certainty with that foot of yours."

"Thank you," I answered. Or at least I tried to. I choked on the words.

What had I done? But there was no time for second thoughts. I darted back up on deck and onto the dock. My pack was tucked away in the back of Vulgrin's stall. My journal, quills and inkhorn were in it and I always kept it with me for safety's sake. Vulgrin had not yet arrived. I helped myself to three of his finest skins, stuffed them in my pack as well, filled my inkhorn to the brim and stole two new quills. Then I raced back to the ship.

So here I am. Curled in a corner on a bed of straw, surrounded by forty warhorses and two palfreys. What will Vulgrin think when he realizes I have disappeared? I care not a whit. He'll probably be relieved to be rid of me. But possibly not. I did work hard for him—until the crusaders came anyway. He will be furious when he discovers the missing skins and quills.

Luckily I gave my goat to Mistress Matilde yesterday. I was feeling so wretched at the thought of the crusaders leaving and knew I would have no more use for the nanny, so I decided that Mistress Matilde might as well have her to keep on giving milk for her children and her cheeses. I suppose she is on a ship too, heading for the Holy Land.

Heading for the Holy Land. I still cannot truly believe it!

The smell is already very ripe down here though. The ship is rolling with the motion of the sea. I hear waves slapping against the sides. It is difficult to write, but I can manage. I must confess, my stomach does not like this at all. In fact, I think I must stop writing for I am about to be sick. Again. Perhaps I should not have been so disdainful of King Philip when he was seasick.

The twelfth day of April

This morning I heard from one of the other soldiers that Sebrand also was as sick as a dog and could not move from his pallet amidships. The opportunity was too good to miss. I determined that no matter how I felt, I would go up onto the deck and see what there was to see. Now that I am embarked on this great adventure I'm not going to miss a bit of it.

What a sight there was! I am still very ill and the ship is tossing so violently that I can barely write, but I must tell of this. I had a hard time dodging the sailors as they scrambled around the decks and the rigging. Some swore at me to get out of the way, but one of them was a bit more friendly and answered my questions when I dared to ask. Even he laughed at my open-mouthed awe, however, and I'm sure he thought me a great landlubberly fool.

There must be over two hundred ships in this fleet—galleys such as I have often seen in our harbor and other long, narrow warships that have a deadly look about them. Some of the ships have their prows coated with iron. For ramming, the sailor told me. All are being driven by oars as well as sails, and when I wondered why, he said it was to make the most speed possible at this beginning of our journey.

There are ships around us and behind us as far as the eye can see. The ocean is alive with them. King Richard's ship leads and his royal blue and gold pennant streams back in the wind. It is a dromond—the largest of the warships. The ship I am on is also a dromond and we follow close behind him. The rest follow us.

The wind blows hard, so strong that it nearly knocked me down. The deck is slippery with sea spray too, and I was forced to grab for handholds in order to keep upright. I was determined not to fall and make myself a laughingstock in front of the sailors.

Our ship is packed to the scuppers with men and supplies. There are the sailors who man the oars and the others who climb up the rigging like spiders to tend the sails. As well there are about forty knights and forty more soldiers from King Richard's army. The knights hold themselves apart from the ordinary soldiers, of course, and have taken over most of the stern of the ship. They were nowhere to be seen when I was on deck. I imagine they were below, as sick as the rest of us. The soldiers sleep mostly on the deck and are fitted in as tightly as possible. Already there have been fights and brawls, and the scuppers are awash with vomit and filth. I think I am lucky to have only horses as companions.

The two noble ladies keep to their cabin. I wonder if they will come out at all on this voyage.

Men from the ships shout to each other constantly and blow trumpets in order to keep the vessels in touch. At night, I am told, a great lantern hangs from King Richard's masthead to serve as a guide to the rest.

I was particularly impressed by the oarsmen. They sit in the belly of the ship, pulling on the massive oars in time to a beat set by a boatsman, who stands before them with a huge drum. All the time I watched, their eyes never left him and they never missed a beat.

There was so much to see and take in. Too much. I have lived on an island with water around me all my life, yet never could I have imagined the vastness of this sea. Nothing but heaving waves, melting into a rolling, shifting horizon no matter which way I turned. It made me feel so small.

I took advantage of being on deck to vomit over the side instead of into the bilges where I sleep. Then I came back down here. Truly, this must be one of the greatest armadas ever assembled. And I am part of it. Sick to death, but part of it nonetheless.

The thirteenth day of April

It is Good Friday. We were told that the priests
would say mass on deck and we could all attend,
but a storm has come up and the ship is rolling and
pitching so violently that we are unable to do so. I
managed to get as far as the top of the ladder, but
then a blast of spray sent me sprawling back down.
The wind howls through the rigging. No man can
possibly be heard from one ship to another now, no
matter how loudly he shouts or blows his trumpet.
Nor can the crews see each other through the
driving rain. How will we ever stay together?

The fifteenth day of April

Easter Sunday. We are still being battered by the
storm. It is impossible for any except the sailors who
have to control the ship to go up on deck, so now
King Richard's men are packed in around me and
the horses. At first the soldiers were rowdy and
noisy, but they have grown quieter and quieter.
They huddle in every available spot, retching. The
only other sound to be heard from them is a weak
curse now and then. Sebrand came below, swearing,
and told us we have lost sight of the other ships. The
priests have also managed to make their way
amongst us and have exhorted us to pray to the risen
Lord who walked on water and stilled the storm.

When will He still this one? Surely the ship cannot
take much more. The sea pours in and the bilges
swim with water. The horses are terrified, as am I.
But I cannot cower in a corner this time. There are
several other men assigned to care for the horses as

well as me, and it takes all of us to keep the animals from stampeding and kicking each other and the men around them to death. The soldiers are very much in the way and a nuisance. The smell of vomit and excrement, both human and animal, is so foul that I try not to breathe. Indeed, the air is so bad that it is hard to do so. It feels like trying to breathe through a thick, stinking broth.

I am certain I will never be able to read what I now write. The ink sloshes and spills out of the horn with every lurch of the ship and I have broken two quills. At least the men around me are too ill to wonder at what I am doing, scribbling away here.

I am trying not to think that this might be the end of us all. And so soon! I haven't seen anything yet.

The seventeeth day of April

The storm has died down. This morning the wind dropped. I thought we were safe and I was starting to care for the horses, even though the ship was still tossing in the waves, when I heard the sailors making a great hue and cry. There was a great deal of running back and forth above deck. Finally I heard the sound of the anchor being dropped. As soon as the soldiers heard that they raced to climb the ladders onto the deck. I was tempted to join them but the horses needed tending and the others who were supposed to do it had deserted as well, so I fed the animals and did my best to keep my feet under me and to calm them. Then I finally scrambled up the ladder to have a look. All the soldiers and sailors were crowded at the railings, gawking, but I managed to squeeze between them and find a space for myself.

We are anchored in a small bay. I could see land with white cliffs and a beach not far off. Just to one side of us the sea crashes into a wall of jagged boulders. It seems we narrowly missed being driven onto them. I shuddered as I looked at the foam-crested waves all hurling themselves onto the rocks. I could just imagine the ship breaking up like kindling wood in that chaos. That would have been the end of us all, I'm certain. I asked the sailor beside me where we were, but he just shrugged.

"You mean you don't know?" I insisted.

He scowled at me so fiercely I did not dare ask anything further. But from the murmurings around me, and the uncertain looks on the men's faces, I could tell that *no one* knew where we were. Worse, not one other ship has come into sight. We are completely lost and alone.

Just before I came back down below deck I saw Queen Joanna. Princess Berengaria has not stirred from her cabin, but Queen Joanna came out of her quarters at the stern of the ship and stood at the railing for a short time. I knew it was she because of her hair. It was as golden and shining as King Richard's. Princess Berengaria, I hear, is dark-haired. The queen was holding a shawl closely wrapped around her shoulders and gazing toward the land. She is a stately lady and would be very beautiful if she looked not so pale and worried.

The eighteenth day of April

All has been quiet. Too quiet. It seems strange that no one has come out to us from the land. We can see a town in the distance and the people there must surely see us, but none have made any effort to contact us.

Sebrand has been ordered to go ashore in a boat with a few of his most trusted men. I know which boat he will take. It is quite large and there is a cover all bundled up at one end. Just enough of a cover to conceal a boy. I burn with curiosity to know what country we have landed in and what is going on here. I wonder if I dare . . .

The twentieth day of April

What a tale I have to tell today! I will have to sharpen my quill extra well for this long story.

Well before dawn this morning I screwed up my courage and crept to the boat that Sebrand would be using to go ashore. I was determined to hide myself in it and see for myself where we were. I was fairly certain that I could get away with this scheme.

I had to step over several sleeping bodies to get there and I accidentally trod on one soldier's hand. For a moment I froze with fear, but all he did was grunt and roll over. I suppose the men get used to being stepped on, sleeping on the deck as they do. When I reached the boat I glanced quickly around to make certain that no one was watching, then, as fast as I could, I clambered over the side and hid myself under the canvas in the bow. Just in time too, as no sooner had I pulled the cover over me than I heard the sailor on watch tramp by. He didn't seem as concerned as I had been about avoiding the sleeping men. A whole chorus of yelps and oaths followed his path.

As I lay there in the dark waiting, my stomach tied itself in knots again, but not with seasickness this time, for I'm over that now. This time it was fear—Sebrand has been friendly to me but he allowed me to come on board only if I stayed out of the way. If he caught me in this escapade he would most certainly be furious. The consequences of what I was doing did not bear thinking of, so I didn't. Instead I concentrated on burrowing in as tightly as I could, strewing ropes and other bits and pieces over me. I chose things with sharp edges so that no one would be tempted to sit on me.

I had a very bad time of it while they hoisted the boat and lowered it overboard. In fact, when it hit the water I was bounced around so much that I nearly cried out. The sharp and pointy objects strewn on top of me proved to be a mistake. They poked through the canvas and I have a mass of cuts and bruises to show for it. I don't care, however, because my plan worked.

Once the boat was launched two sailors leaped in to man the oars. Sebrand and two of his fellow soldiers lumbered in after them. I could hear them cursing and swearing as they stumbled around in the rocking boat. Finally all were organized and the sailors settled in to rowing. It was only a short haul to the beach, and as the seas had calmed somewhat they soon ground the prow on the shore. Then I had a moment of panic. What if the sailors remained with the boat? At that point I heard Sebrand's voice: "Be back before noonday. We'll return to the ship then."

That was a relief. From the sound of it the sailors took off even before Sebrand and his men left. I lay absolutely still, almost without breathing, until all their voices had died away. Then, cautiously, I peeked out.

The beach was deserted. I threw back the canvas and scuttled out of the boat as quickly as I could. I glanced up at the sun and made note of its position. I had to be certain to be back before the men returned. I could see the city walls ahead of me and made for them, praying that the gates would not be shut.

It was very strange. As I walked I swear I could feel the solid land heaving beneath my feet. I had just got used to the rolling and pitching of the ship, it seemed, and now the land was unfamiliar to me. The feeling wore off after an hour or two, however.

In the event, the gates were wide open and there was such a bustle of people going in and out that no one took any notice of me at all. In minutes, I was within the town.

I looked around me with curiosity. The people appeared much the same as the people from my own country—a mixture of races. I heard the same babble of tongues. French, Arabic, Greek, as well as some dialects I could not identify. I had no idea where Sebrand and his men had gone, so I kept a wary eye out for them. It must have been market day because the streets were full of stalls with people selling all manner of wares. The smell of the food cooking reached right down inside me and twisted my stomach. It was no longer queasy and began to remind me that I had not eaten for days. I had no coins, however, so I tightened the rope around the waist of my tunic and went on exploring. Finally I summoned up the courage to approach an old lady who looked fairly friendly. I took the chance of addressing her in Greek.

"I beg you, mistress, could you tell me what city this is?" I asked.

She looked at me as if I had taken leave of my senses, but she understood and replied in the same tongue.

"Know you not where you are?" she asked.

I smiled, a simpering grin, and tried to look foolish and simpleminded. It must have worked, for her face softened.

"It is Limassol, lad. On the island of Cyprus." Then suddenly her eyes narrowed. "You wouldn't be one of the foreigners off that warship, would you now?"

I opened my eyes as wide as I could. "Ship?" I asked. "What ship, mistress?"

"Oh, get on with you," she snapped. "I've no time for simpletons."

It seems she wasn't quite as friendly as I had thought, but that was probably just as well.

Limassol. On the island of Cyprus. I had heard of this land, but certainly never thought I would ever see it.

I determined to explore as much as I could in the

short time I had before I had to get back to the boat. The city is a pretty one and the day was fair. It was warm and the breeze that blew in from the sea was welcome. It carried all manner of foreign and exciting smells on it. I overlooked the background stink of garbage and began to enjoy myself.

Just when I was beginning to think of returning to the boat I found myself in a small back alley. It was a poor lane. The cobblestones were littered with refuse and no one had made any effort to clean it up. The houses on either side were little more than hovels and there were no pleasant smells here at all. It stank even worse than the butchers' alley back home in Messina. A few men lounged in doorways and stared at me in an exceedingly suspicious and unfriendly way. I had just about decided that I would do better to turn around and get away from there when a building at the end caught my eye. It looked like a stockade. A fence surrounded it and through the fence I could see soldiers. Some were lying on the ground, others pacing around. What caught my eye was their dress. They were wearing the colors of King Richard's army! Forgetting all caution I ran to the fence and put my face to an opening.

"Sirs," I hissed, "who are you?"

One of the men whirled to face me. "Who are *you*?" he growled. "What manner of rat is whispering at our prison walls?"

"Are you King Richard's men?" I asked. Then what he said sank in. "Have you been taken captive?" I was confused. Where had these men come from and why were they being held prisoner?

I was ready to bombard the man with more questions, but he forestalled me.

"I don't answer questions from street urchins," he snarled and started to turn away.

"Wait!" I called out, too loudly. I cringed back and cast a quick look over my shoulder to see if anyone had taken notice. A few curious glances were being cast my way.

"Wait," I called again, more softly but just as urgently. I had to find out what was going on. "I am one of King Richard's men too. From Queen Joanna's ship," I said, lying only a little. That got his attention. He whirled back to face me.

"Queen Joanna's ship?" he snapped. "Where is it?"

"Offshore. Anchored in the bay," I told him.

He came over to the fence and motioned me closer. "Who has come ashore from your ship?" he asked.

"Only a small party of soldiers and myself," I replied. I looked over my shoulder again. Most of the men were still ignoring me, but two of them had straightened up and seemed to be taking an interest.

"Get back to your ship as quickly as you can and tell your masters not to let anyone else off it. These Cypriots are capturing any of King Richard's men they can lay hold of and holding them prisoner. Most especially, tell them to guard the queen. She would be a prize beyond compare to Emperor Isaac Commenus, who rules here. Is the king's ship here too?"

"No," I answered. "Only the queen's. From

whence came you?" I was burning with curiosity, even though I could see the Cypriots beginning to move in my direction.

"We are from two ships that were wrecked just along the shore from here. Some of us survived and made our way ashore, only to be taken captive. Warn your masters. Warn the queen!"

At that moment a voice called out from within the stockade. The man stumbled as he turned quickly away from the fence. Only then did I see that blood stained one sleeve and his left arm hung useless at his side.

Two townsmen were approaching. I did not wait to see anything else, but took to my heels as fast as I could. One of them yelled something after me, but I paid no heed. I did not stop running until I had escaped the gates of the city and reached the boat. I was just in time. No sooner had I hidden myself under the canvas when first the sailors, then Sebrand and his men, came back. I was relieved to hear them. I feared that they too might have been taken prisoner. It seemed they had met with an altogether different reception, however.

"A cordial lot," I heard Sebrand say. Under the canvas, my eyebrows shot up in surprise. "I will report to the queen all that they told me and relay their invitation to her to come ashore and stay in more hospitable quarters until King Richard can be found."

God help us, I thought. So that is why they let him go free. He has been well and truly duped.

They will take Queen Joanna prisoner and hold her for ransom! I had to warn the queen, but how?

I puzzled over it all during the choppy ride back to the ship. So concerned was I that I forgot to worry about my own safety when our boat was hoisted back aboard. I received a fair knocking about, but I was too busy thinking to let it bother me.

I could not go to Sebrand and tell him what I had discovered. He would be furious with me for stowing away and deceiving him in such a fashion. He would surely think, and perhaps rightly so I must admit, that my actions were poor thanks for the favor he had done me in allowing me to come along. But I had to do something. The danger to the queen—and to the rest of us as well—was too great. If she were taken hostage I did not doubt the Cypriots would attack the ship itself, and then what would happen? I certainly had no wish to be taken prisoner—or killed!

My brain tore at the problem, going first one way and then another. Suddenly the memory of Queen Joanna standing at the railing came back to me. She had looked kind. What if I went straight to her? She was bound to come out for air this evening again— I could lie in wait and accost her then.

The twenty-first day of April

I had to stop writing last night. My wick sputtered out and my quill broke. I will continue my tale now. It is so wondrous that I must set it down. I, Matthew of Messina, the lowliest of brats as I have so often been told, have actually talked to a queen! This is how it came to pass.

I tended to the horses and fulfilled my duties for the rest of the day yesterday and kept as quiet as a mouse, although I was most desperately anxious. I knew that Sebrand had reported to the queen soon after we returned, and I could only pray that she would not embark for the shore before I had a chance to speak to her.

As soon as the horses were fed and watered for the night I climbed back up the ladder. Luckily Sebrand was nowhere in sight, and the sailors are so used to my scuttling around now that they pay me no attention at all. My heart took a huge leap as I saw Queen Joanna pacing the deck in the stern. Her face looked even more troubled than before. I crept along the deck toward her, keeping a sharp lookout for anyone who might stop me. Within minutes I was close enough to her to speak. She was even more beautiful than I had thought. She was dressed in a gown of blue, dark as midnight, that shimmered in the light of a lantern hanging from the mast. The evening air was cool and she clasped a light shawl around her shoulders. Her hair was unbound and fell loosely around her shoulders. Never have I been so close to one so lovely. I drank in every detail.

Seeing her standing there, my tongue seemed to cleave to the roof of my mouth. How could I possibly dare to speak to such a great lady? Then I remembered what would happen if I did not.

"Your Grace," I whispered. "May I speak with you?"

She started as if woken from a dream and looked around, not seeing me at first.

"Who is there?" she asked.

"My name is Matthew," I answered, keeping my voice low. "I care for the horses."

She frowned. "Come into the light, boy. What are you doing here and why do you dare speak to me?"

For a moment I almost turned and ran, but then I took a deep breath and mustered my courage.

"I was in the town today, Your Grace," I said with a gulp. "I saw men from two of King Richard's ships imprisoned in a stockade." Now that I had started my tongue almost ran away with me in my haste to say what I had to before she sent me away—or worse, called someone to take me away.

"I spoke with one of the men and he told me to warn you that Emperor Isaac Commenus is a liar. He has captured the survivors of two of King Richard's ships that foundered down the shore from here." The words all tumbled out in one breath and I was forced to stop for air.

Queen Joanna looked at me. Her frown deepened.

"Your officer has just told me that this Isaac Commenus has offered me accommodation and shelter ashore," she said.

"It is a trick, Your Grace," I said. I know I sounded desperate. "He means to take you hostage."

"Why should I believe you, a mere stableboy, and not your officer?" she asked.

"Sebrand has been tricked as well," I answered. I

had to make her believe me. "I am telling the truth, Your Grace. I spoke to the prisoners myself."

She stared hard at me. I felt as if her eyes were looking right inside my head. It took all my will not to drop my gaze from hers. Finally, as if coming to a decision, she gave a little nod. "I have heard before that Isaac Commenus is a tricky and devious man. He was sent here as a governor for the Byzantine Empire, but now, it would seem, styles himself emperor." She paused and looked thoughtfully shoreward, then faced me again. "Go back to your horses, boy. I will consider what you've told me."

I turned to go and then stopped. There was one thing more. Did I dare ask her?

"Your Grace," I said, "could you please not tell the officer that it was I who warned you?"

In the light from the lantern I saw one eyebrow lift. I swear her mouth quirked in the beginnings of a smile.

"So," she said, "you went ashore without permission. How, I wonder, did you accomplish that?"

I hung my head. I was certainly not going to answer that question.

"Go," she repeated. "I do not have to explain my decisions to soldiers. I will keep your secret."

So here I am. All I can do now is pray that she will believe me and stay on board this ship.

The twenty-second day of April

Queen Joanna did not accept the emperor's invitation. She asked instead for permission for our crew to go ashore to buy food and wine, but that request was refused. It is clear enough now that we are not amongst friends.

The thirtieth day of April

Still no sign of King Richard. He must be searching for us, especially when his sister and his intended bride are on board this ship. Sebrand told us that our ship is also loaded with treasure—probably the dowry that King Richard forced King Tancred to return to him. What will happen to us if Isaac Commenus hears of that, I wonder.

The sixth day of May

King Richard has arrived! The whole fleet appeared over the horizon just before sunset. A welcome sight indeed. With their sails filling the sky the ships looked like a great flock of gulls swooping in. We are surrounded now by dromonds and galleys, and King Richard has summoned Queen Joanna and Princess Berengaria to his ship.

The seventh day of May

King Richard has demanded that Emperor Isaac Commenus release his men and give back the loot he stole from the wrecked ships. The emperor has refused. I wonder if he has heard what happened to King Tancred when he crossed the English king.

The eighth day of May

We are preparing for war, but so is Isaac Commenus. On the beach we can see an immense barricade being thrown up. I have been watching all morning. The emperor's men are hauling out old barrels, casks, doors, window frames, shutters—whatever they can lay their hands on, it seems. They have even piled pieces of wrecked ships and planks and benches on the sands. Every kind of debris imaginable is piled up on that beach. It makes a formidable barrier for King Richard's men to break through. As well, no fewer than five Greek war galleys have sailed out from the harbor and positioned themselves between us and the shore.

It has been raining for the past two days, but this morning the sun broke through and shone directly down on the castle of Limassol. The castle looms high on a rocky hill overlooking the city and shines like a beacon in the sunlight. It seems so strong and impregnable, but if anyone can take it I am certain King Richard will.

The king is readying a small armada of little boats. His horses will be useless to him here, I fear, as there is no way of transporting them to shore. The atmosphere on the ship is tense.

The ninth day of May

The battle is over and what a battle it was. My fingers still tremble so that I can hardly write. I watched from the rail of the ship. The queen herself also watched, as did Princess Berengaria, but they did not see me. I made certain to keep hidden from view behind a pile of crates. The princess looks to be very young. Probably not much older than I.

With the first light of dawn King Richard's knights and soldiers crowded into the small boats.

The men made hard work of clambering down the ropes and getting themselves into the cockleshell crafts, weighed down as they were by their armor and weapons. I could only pray that no boats would capsize as, if they did, the men would surely drown. The king himself led in the first boat.

I held my breath as I watched them sail straight toward the five war galleys. Then, in each of King Richard's small boats, crossbowmen stood up and began to fire. These English crossbowmen are said to be the best in the world and I now believe it. Never have I seen such a hail of arrows. Some bore flaming torches and soon the galleys were all ablaze. It was all I could do to restrain a cheer, but I kept silent, not wanting to draw attention to myself.

The fire was so devastating that the sailors were forced to abandon their ships and launched themselves into the water. The screams of drowning and dying men filled the air and the cheer I had been suppressing with so much difficulty died in my throat. I cast a quick glance at the queen and Princess Berengaria. Queen Joanna's knuckles were white against the dark wood of the rail, but she stood fast, her face grim. The princess let out a small cry, however, and ran for her cabin. I could see her eyes big with horror.

Then I turned my attention back to the king's boats. The oarsmen were putting such effort behind their strokes that the little crafts flew over the waves. The king was the first off. He leaped out of his boat before it had fairly made the shore and landed in water up to his hips. It slowed him down not a bit. He charged toward the emperor's army, brandishing his sword and bellowing at the top of his lungs. His knights followed, shouting as well and lashing the water into a frenzy. They made short work of hacking a way through the barricades although they were under a constant hail of arrows themselves. I heard men scream and saw them fall to the right and the left of King Richard, but he forged ahead untouched, as if divinely protected. The Greeks made a feeble attempt to stop the attacking army after it had torn through the barricades, but the English soldiers pushed them back ruthlessly.

A flash of color caught my eye. One of the Greek nobles, richly dressed in a golden tunic, raced for a horse and leaped upon its back. He wrenched the animal around and made a run for the city. King Richard saw him too. Spying another riderless horse, he grabbed its reins and hoisted himself onto its back, then galloped after him. A shout came loud and clear over all the other noise of battle: "Come, Emperor! Come and joust with me!"

But the noble, who I now realized was none other than Isaac Commenus himself, was having none of it. His was the faster horse and he disappeared into the distance.

After that the emperor's army broke and ran. The town of Limassol and the castle that looked so unassailable are now King Richard's.

I have to stop here. I am full of distressing thoughts. The battle was glorious. Exciting. It did not terrify me as did the conflict for Messina, probably because I was watching from a safe distance. But once again it was a war against our fellow Christians.

The tenth day of May

We have beached the ships and landed the horses. It is lucky that Sebrand did allow me to stay with the ship, for they could never have done it without my help. Perhaps I sound immodest, but it is true. I have a way with those horses that rough soldiers do not.

As soon as camp was set up on the shore King Richard and most of his army mounted and thundered off after the emperor. We await news.

The eleventh day of May

And the news is good yet again. The king's army surrounded the Cypriots' camp and quickly took it, but unfortunately the emperor escaped once more. A very slippery sort of person, he is.

There was even more excitement today. King Guy of Jerusalem arrived. Three galleys were sighted early this morning and put the whole camp into a tizzy. We all ran down to the shore, duties forgotten. As soon as the galleys were berthed, a clutch of lavishly dressed nobles came ashore. They turned out to be King Guy himself, his brother Geoffrey of Lusignan, Humphrey of Toron, Bohemond, the prince of Antioch, Raymond, the count of Tripoli, Leon, the brother of the prince of Armenia and a number of others. The most important men in the Holy Land, I am assured by the priest who poured all this information into my ear.

King Guy is an impressive figure although, mind you, he is not king of very much. He has lost Jerusalem and most of the rest of his kingdom to

Salah-ud-Din. Helping him to regain Jerusalem and the rest of his lost Christian kingdom is the very reason for this crusade, but he does not have the air of a man who is humbly grateful.

The twelfth day of May

King Richard married Princess Berengaria today, and King Guy and the other nobles of Ôutremer were honored guests. There was great feasting in the camp to celebrate. Again, I was able to eat until I nearly burst. I was more careful with the wine though.

The marriage took place in the chapel of the castle of Limassol, and then the princess was crowned queen by no less than the Bishop of Evreux. (He is a Norman, like my father.) I saw the princess as she rode past in procession on her way to the chapel. The street was lined with cheering people and this time I, of course, was cheering as loudly as the rest. The princess did not smile or wave back, however. She rode with her eyes cast down and her fingers tight on the reins of her palfrey. I could see that she was biting her lip. I wonder what it would be like to be a young maid sold into marriage to a strange man, in a strange country—and to go off to war for a bridal trip. But that is the way of it with kings and queens. They do what is good for their countries and make such alliances as necessary. It has always been so, I suppose, and probably always will be so.

Strange, I have never thought so closely on these matters before. But then I have never been so close to kings and queens and princesses before either.

The king sent wine to the marketplace in the city and great quantities of food, so the townspeople are celebrating as well. No one seems to miss the emperor.

The fourteenth day of May

Celebrations continue in the town. From the camp I can see people carousing around the city walls and the music of minstrels drifts down to my ears. Celebrations have ceased here in camp, however, and it is back to work.

The fifteenth day of May

I hardly know how to write this. I have pinched myself so often to be sure I am not dreaming that my arms are mottled and blue. Let me gather my wits and start at the beginning.

Barely had I finished scribbling those last lines yesterday when a soldier poked his head around the shelter I have built for myself near the horses.

"Are you the boy called Matthew?" he bellowed.

"I am," I answered and my insides suddenly went all hollow. What trouble was coming to me now?

"Get up then and follow me," he commanded.

I stuffed my inkhorn and skins into my sack and hid it quickly under a pile of branches.

"Hurry up!" the soldier barked. "Do you think to keep the king waiting, a miserable little cur such as yourself?"

My breath left my body in a rush and I would have fallen if there had been time. The king!

The soldier grabbed me by the elbow and hauled me out, then dragged me, trotting lop-footedly, across the camp to the king's own pavilion. At the entrance flap he let me go.

"This is the boy the king would see," he said to a guard who stood stiffly beside the opening.

The guard stepped aside. I do not think I would have been able to move if the soldier had not grasped me again and pushed me forward. As it was I stumbled over the threshold and almost fell. I collected myself and looked up. Sitting in front of me was the Lionheart himself and beside him was Queen Joanna. Of Princess Berengaria, now Queen Berengaria, there was no sign. I must have looked terrified because Queen Joanna smiled at me and spoke.

"Do not be afraid, Matthew," she said. Her voice was as sweet as I remembered. She was dressed in a gown of purest white.

"You did us a great service, Matthew," the king said.

A great service? What was he talking about? I dared a sideways glance.

"You warned the queen against going ashore. If she had accepted the invitation, she would no doubt at this moment be a hostage and we would not have been able to assault and capture this city. We owe you much, lad," he said.

"Look up, Matthew. You have nothing to fear here. We have called you here to thank you." Queen Joanna's voice encouraged me to look straight at her. But I still did not dare look at the king.

"We would reward you," King Richard said. "What would your wish be?"

I tried to speak but found to my horror that I had no voice. My tongue clacked against my teeth but no sound came out.

"Speak, Matthew," the queen encouraged. "What would you wish as compensation for your help to me?"

"I . . ." The word sounded like the grunt a pig would make. I flushed and tried again. "I wish only to serve you, Sire." Finally I dared to meet his gaze.

"To serve me. Hmmm." The king raised an eyebrow. "And what do you now, boy?"

"I tend the horses, Sire," I said.

"What else can you do?" His words whipped out at me.

What could I say? I flushed so red that my face felt as if it would explode. How had I the nerve to offer to serve King Richard of England? What could I, a miserable cripple, do for such a majesty? I cast about desperately in my mind, and then—I do not even know now what possessed me to say it, I blurted out, "I can write, Sire. I am a scribe."

"A scribe!" Both royal eyebrows rose. "And in what languages can you write, my young scribe?"

"French, Sire. And Latin. And a little Greek." The words began to pour out of my mouth without my being able to control them. "And English, Sire."

"English! Pah! A language for peasants. I don't care for English. But if you are telling the truth— you are, boy, aren't you?" He frowned at me suddenly and his eyes turned into blue ice. I would not want to face those eyes on a battlefield.

"Yes, Sire," I stuttered. "I can speak and write in all those languages. And I speak Arabic too, although I cannot write it. And I write well, Sire. I am a good scribe." Whatever prompted me to make that claim I will never know. I was horrified to hear myself saying it. I tensed every muscle in my body and waited for his anger. How dare I boast to the king of England?

The eyebrows rose even higher. Then suddenly the king's face broke into a smile. He laughed.

"A confident little cripple you are, aren't you?" he said with a chortle. "Well, boy, I'll put you to the test. One of my scribes was lost in the storm, a man of little importance, but his loss is onerous to me. He tallied shipments, kept count of goods used and purchased—or seized," he added with a wry smile. "That sort of thing. Could you do that?"

"Oh, yes, Sire. Indeed I could, Sire." My words tripped over each other in my eagerness. Truly, I would have affirmed that I could do anything he asked, no matter what it might have been.

"Well, then. We'll set you up in a tent near mine and you can be my junior scribe. I need a list of the supplies we've found in the castle to begin with, and who knows—if you truly are as good as you think you are—perhaps I'll find other uses for you. Do you want to go on crusade?" This last he barked with a return of the frown.

"I do, Sire," I answered, trying to stop myself from babbling and to regain some semblance of dignity. I do not think I succeeded too well.

"Then on crusade you will go." He snapped his fingers and a soldier appeared. "Find shelter for this boy. He will attend me every morning to do my bidding." He stopped and looked more closely at me. "And for mercy's sake, wash him and find him some decent clothing. God's legs, but the boy is filthy!"

So here I am. Cleaner than I have ever been in my life (although I did not see the need for quite so much cold water and scrubbing) and in my own tent! I managed to sneak back to my old shelter for my skins and inkhorn, but the king himself said that he would give me parchments and ink of the very best quality to write with.

Now I think it very lucky that Vulgrin was so hard with me. As well, writing this journal has not only improved my hand but has taught me much about the art of putting words together. I will keep on with it. As I write in English, it is not likely anyone would be able to read this journal if they did find it. The nobles do not speak English—mostly French and Latin as does the king—and the English soldiers cannot read. I liked the horses, though, and I shall miss tending them.

The seventeeth day of May

My new life is proving interesting. I reported to the king this morning and then promptly set about listing all the supplies in the castle. This task will take a while. While I was with the king, however, who should appear but Emperor Isaac Commenus himself! King Richard greeted him civilly, hiding his surprise most wonderfully, I thought, and invited him to dine. Just days ago he had been chasing the emperor all over the island of Cyprus! I melted into the background and tried to look as much like one of the tapestries as possible so as to hear all they said, but to my chagrin the king remembered my presence.

"Off to your duties, boy," he commanded and I was forced to leave. I heard what happened later, however, from one of the guards. His name is Rigord and he is adept at listening through entrance curtains. I shall have to curry his favor.

I am learning much about how to get information out of people, by the way. It is a useful talent.

Rigord said that the king and the emperor came to an agreement that Isaac Commenus would swear allegiance to King Richard and come on crusade with him with five hundred knights. He also promised to hand over the castles of Cyprus as a pledge of his sincerity, as well as three thousand, five hundred marks. Rigord says he knew the emperor was lying all along, and it seems he was right. After the king and Isaac Commenus finished their meal, the emperor snuck out, mounted his horse—which is called Fauvel and is famous for its speed and endurance, I hear—and disappeared into the night. He was obviously just sounding the king out and had not the slightest intention of keeping his promises. The king feels he has been made a fool of and is furious, Rigord says, and is preparing to pursue the emperor. I do not think it wise to make a fool of the king of England.

The eighteenth day of May

Rigord is proving to be as forthcoming as a gushing spring. I have taken to cleaning his armor for him and sharpening his spear. It loosens his tongue marvelously.

The latest gossip is that King Philip has arrived in the Holy Land and is already causing trouble. He is campaigning to replace Guy, the rightful king of Jerusalem, with Conrad of Montferrat, Lord of Tyre.

God's legs, but these nobles do love their intrigues! ("God's legs" is King Richard's favorite oath and I have decided to adopt it myself.)

The nineteenth day of May

They have all sailed off together to find the emperor. I am left with my listing. It is very boring. I miss the horses.

The thirtieth day of May

Another great victory. Not only did King Richard capture the emperor, but he and King Guy went on to conquer the whole of Cyprus. Now King Richard is lord of Cyprus and all the riches of the island are his. This victory will give the armies in Ôutremer a good source of supplies. Rigord, who was on the campaign, said that the citizens of Cyprus recognized King Richard as their liege lord gleefully. I am not so certain of that, as the king required the men to shave off their beards so as to prove their loyalty and look more like westerners. These Greeks are proud of their hairy faces—I wonder just how gleeful they really are.

The emperor was brought back in chains and there is a story there too. It seems—according to Rigord, of course—that part of the terms of Isaac Commenus's surrender was that he not be put in iron chains. King Richard agreed, and then, after the emperor had surrendered, had him put in *silver* chains! He will be sent to Syria as a prisoner. Apparently there is more than one way to keep your word and your honor if you are a king.

And I was right, it doesn't do to make a fool of the king of England.

The fifth day of June

At last! We set sail this morning for Ôutremer! This time it is very different for me. I have a nook to myself near the king's cabin on his own ship. King Richard was pleased with my work on Cyprus and has promised to give me more, although so far I have had nothing to do. Just as well, as I am so excited I can hardly write. I must go and hang over the rail so I do not miss my first glimpse of the Holy Land.

The sixth day of June

We reached Tyre today and disembarked with all eagerness, only to find that the garrison, acting on instructions from King Philip and Conrad of Montferrat—he who would be king of Jerusalem—would not give King Richard permission to enter the town. This is almost treason. The king is beside himself with anger. I have never seen him in such a state. We are camped outside the walls and King Richard rages within his tent. His voice carries to every part of the camp—inside the city walls as well, I would wager—and the rest of us are cowering and trying to keep out of his way.

Tomorrow we will sail southward down the coast to Acre. What will we find there?

The seventh day of June

What excitement today and what an odd outcome! We set sail from Tyre early in the morning. The king did not summon me to him, so I was free to hang over the rail to my heart's content. I think I was born to be a sailor. Now that I am no longer seasick, I relish the motion of the ship when she is under sail and speeding through the waves so quickly, with no need of the oarsmen. The wind whistles through the rigging and fills my body with its freshness. Truly, when I am on deck I feel as if I were made entirely of air and sun and salt spray.

While I was clinging to the rail, drinking in every drop of this wonderful day, I suddenly saw a silvery flash upon the water. Then another. And another. To my utter astonishment, small fish were hurling themselves out of the waves and *flying* through the air for incredible distances before flopping back in. In my excitement I cried aloud to the sailor nearest me.

"Look!" I shouted. "Fish! Flying!"

He didn't even bother to raise his head from the frayed rope he was repairing.

"See them all the time," he said, sounding bored. "Nothing special about them."

I was very embarrassed.

Then I saw another fish, much bigger, leap out of the water in an arc and dive back in. I wasn't about to display my ignorance again, so I kept quiet this time and just watched. There were about three of the huge creatures and I could swear they were following alongside us and playing! I did learn later by asking another sailor a few casual questions that these fish are called dolphins and they often follow ships at sea. They seem to enjoy human company, he said. Indeed, he swore that some of these fish once saved a shipwrecked man. The man was clinging to a piece of wreckage when he was encircled by a group of them. At first he screamed in terror, believing they were about to eat him, but then, to his amazement, the dolphins began to nose his plank toward shore. They pushed him all the way in, then gave a few joyous leaps and disappeared back out to sea. It is a marvelous tale. I am not certain I believe it, but I will be on the watch for these creatures and I hope I see more of them.

As I was watching the flying fish I heard another sailor, high in the rigging, call out, "Sail, ho!"

That brought men scurrying from all parts of the ship. I narrowed my eyes and tried my best to see the other ship, but it was several moments before I could make out the shape of sails against the horizon. The ship seemed to be changing its direction—tacking so that it would avoid us. At that moment the king himself appeared on deck.

"Bring us closer to that ship," he ordered. "I would see what flag she carries."

Immediately more sails were raised and we sped

to intercept the strange vessel. In minutes we were within hailing distance.

"Whence come you?" our captain bellowed.

"We are Genoese, bound for Tyre," came back the answer, fragmented by the wind.

The king frowned. At that one of the sailors came forward. I thought him bold to approach the king without permission, but sailors are an independent lot.

"Hang me, Sire," he said, "if that ship is not Turkish!"

The king looked at the man keenly, then barked, "Have one of our galleys close with that ship!"

The orders were trumpeted out. Oars sprang out from the galley beside us and the oarsmen made haste to close the distance between her and the unknown ship. No sooner did she close with it, however, than a rain of fiery arrows and missiles descended upon her. Undaunted she ran even closer. I could see the sailors preparing to board the enemy ship. They returned the fire with their own arrows and flaming missiles, but in spite of all the efforts of her crew, our galley did not seem able to get close enough to board.

I was fairly dancing at the rail in my frenzy.

Finally, the king's patience seemed to run out.

"Ram her!" he ordered.

One of the iron-prowed warships broke away and headed for the enemy vessel. Through the hail of fire she plowed, her oarsmen not faltering for a moment. I lost all sense of myself and cried out at the top of my voice along with all the rest who were shouting and yelling. Our warship collided with the enemy ship. There was a horrible sound of wood splintering. For one brief moment all seemed silent, then the men on the doomed ship began to scream. Missiles from our first galley landed on her deck and in another instant she was aflame. I could see men hurling themselves into the sea from her rails, even as she began to sink.

The king ordered our ship close in, and ropes were thrown to the survivors in the water. Most of them were pulled out. Some, however, floated unmoving, tossing lifelessly in the waves. I could still hear screams from the other ship. Bits of planking flamed in the sea around us.

Then I saw a boy in the water just below where I stood. He was floundering and thrashing around, and it was clear he could not swim. No one else noticed him, but I don't think he could have reached for a rope even if one had been thrown to him. I watched in horror as he sank beneath the waves. Then I saw a flash of sodden scarlet as he resurfaced briefly. He looked up at me, and in the instant that our eyes met he cried out.

I didn't have time to think. I braced myself on the railing and vaulted over. I may be clumsy on land, but thanks be to God I am a good swimmer!

The cold of the sea shocked me as I plunged into it. The saltwater filled my nostrils and blinded me. For a moment I groped unseeingly for the boy, then my hand touched something solid. I grabbed it and hauled it close and found that I was holding onto the boy's limp body by one arm. I slipped my arm under both of his and brought his head above water. Then I shouted. I shouted more loudly than I have ever shouted before, because at that moment I realized fully what I had done and I was terrified. What if no one saw me? What if the boy began to struggle and pulled me down with him?

I cannot find words to describe how relieved I was when one of the sailors on board our ship saw me. He threw a rope and I made a desperate grab for it. Just then the boy came back to full consciousness. He cried out again and began to struggle, but luckily I had a firm grip on the rope.

"Stop it!" I cried in Arabic, as it was obvious this was indeed a Muslim ship.

He struggled even more fiercely.

"Stop it!" I screamed again. If I had had a free hand I would have hit him, I was so angry. Here I was, trying to save his life and he was putting us both in danger.

At last he seemed to realize he was safe.

"Can you hang onto the rope while they pull you aboard?" I gasped. I was sputtering and swallowing seawater at a great rate. I think I must have had as much of it inside me as he did.

He nodded weakly. He coughed, but reached for the rope and clutched it tightly.

At that moment I realized that the sea around me was full of snakes! I cannot begin to describe the horror that washed over me. Their long, slippery bodies lashed into me as they whipped desperately in the water. One even twined around my arm and I screamed. Just then another rope splashed into the waves beside me and I made a frenzied lunge for it. I was battered against the side of the ship repeatedly as the sailors pulled me up, but I hardly even noticed, so glad was I to reach the safety of the deck again.

It was only then, as I stood there dripping and spitting up seawater, with the boy collapsed on the deck beside me, that I could see him clearly. Long black hair clung wetly to his body, all the way to his waist. He was not wearing men's clothing, but was clad in a soaking wet gown. He was small and thin, and there was no mistaking one thing. He was not a boy. He was a girl!

Later . . .

I had to stop writing as the king called me to tally the goods that we managed to salvage from the Muslim ship. He is certainly a great one for listing his prizes as soon as he gets them!

To continue . . .

I stood there, staring stupidly at the girl, while the sailors crowded around, laughing.

"A maid!" one cried. "We've been given the gift of a maid from the sea!"

"Does she live?" another one asked. He gave the girl's body a jab with his toe. At that she stirred, but her eyes remained closed. Strands of black hair fell wetly across her face.

I started forward. I had no idea what I could do, but I knew I had to do something.

Just at that moment a voice rang out.

"Stand back. Leave that child alone!"

To my surprise Queen Joanna strode forward to stand beside the girl. She and Queen Berengaria sail with the king now, for greater safety, I suppose. The queen looked around and her gaze fastened upon me.

"You, Matthew. Pick up this girl and follow me."

"Yes, Your Grace," I stuttered.

She turned and sailed through the men back to her cabin.

I bent toward the girl.

One of the sailors jostled me. He laughed and made a crude gesture. "We'll carry her for you, gimp foot," he said with a nasty chortle. "Won't we, mates?"

This particular sailor, whose name is Hugh, has ridiculed me ever since I joined this ship. I ignored him, but the men behind him laughed as well and I did not like the sound of it at all. I know these men, and I know full well what would be the fate of a helpless maid in their hands.

"The queen gave an order," I shot back. "It must be obeyed."

"And *you* are the one to do it, gimp foot?" Hugh guffawed. "I wager you couldn't carry a *cat* across this deck with that devil-begotten foot."

That was enough. I gave him as good a glare as I could muster, then bent to pick up the girl.

I couldn't help staggering, even though her body felt as light as my little goat's had. Then I got a better grip on her and slung her over one shoulder. It wasn't very dignified, but it was the only way I could manage. As I did so, she coughed again and a

great flood of water streamed down my back. I was
so wet it did not matter.

I steadied myself against the gentle rolling of the
boat and tried to ignore the sailors who were now
laughing uproariously. I made my way after the
queen. I stumbled several times and almost
dropped the girl twice, but managed to grab onto
something each time and regain my balance. My
foot pained me to the point where I felt I was walking on knives, but I clamped my teeth tight shut and
carried on. I knew I could do this if I wanted to
badly enough, and I did. It may have been just an
oversight, but the queen obviously does not think of
me as a cripple. She may well be the first person in
the world who does not.

Finally I reached the queen's cabin. She stood
waiting for me, holding the door open.

"Put her down there," she ordered, gesturing to a
pile of silken pillows.

"But she is soaking wet, Your Grace," I
protested, "and coughing up filthy water."

"Do as you are told, Matthew," she said sternly.

I hastened to obey.

"Now, leave and send my maidservants to me. I
will take care of her. The poor child is half-
drowned," she added. As she spoke Queen Joanna
knelt beside the girl and began to massage her hands.
The girl whimpered again. Her eyes opened. She
tried to draw back, but the queen held on to her.

Obviously this queen is used to getting her own
way. And she is kind, I know. The little mermaiden
I rescued from the sea will be in good hands.

Who is she? I wonder what she was doing on that ship.

The eighth day of June

I dreamed of snakes and drowning all last night. One of the sailors told me that the Muslim ship had been carrying two hundred of the slithery creatures. The ship was going to reinforce the garrison of Acre that our crusaders were besieging, he said, and they had planned to set the snakes loose in the crusader camp. I am still shuddering.

This morning, after attending upon the king, I received a summons from Queen Joanna. The queen was reclining on a couch piled high with pillows. Behind her a maidservant hovered, her mouth all squinched up as if she had just tasted something bitter. Off to one side stood Father Aimar, the queen's own confessor. He is said to be a most holy man, but is so tall and stern he frightens me somewhat. Beside the queen, on another pile of pillows, crouched the girl I had plucked from the water. At least I presumed it was she. She was dressed in a light shift, lent no doubt by the maidservant (but none too willingly, judging by the look on the servant's face). The girl's hair was dry now and flowed around her shoulders in a sea of black waves. She looked to be about twelve or thirteen years old and it was clear that she was terrified.

"This child will not speak," the queen said. "I have tried to communicate with her, but to no avail. I wish to assure her that she is safe here, that there is no need for her to be so fearful, but she cannot understand me. You said that you could speak many languages, Matthew. Could you try to talk to her?"

"Yes, Your Grace," I replied. "I think she speaks Arabic and I have a good knowledge of that tongue." I furrowed my brow slightly, as Vulgrin used to do when he was trying to impress a rich merchant with the efficiency of his services. I hoped I looked stern and sounded competent. I'm not certain how successful I was, however, as that small smile tweaked at one corner of the queen's mouth again. Nevertheless I drew myself up as tall as I could and turned to the girl.

"Who are you?" I demanded. "What is your name?"

It was not, perhaps, the best approach. The girl's eyes filled with tears and she hid her face in her hands. The queen gave a small cough. I decided a quick change of tactics was in order.

"My name is Matthew," I said more softly. "I am the one who saved you from the sea, remember? Could you not tell me your name?"

She dropped her hands and looked at me. "Where is my father?" she whispered.

"Who is your father?" I countered.

"He is the captain of the ship you attacked."

"He attacked us first," I replied without thinking. Another mistake.

"That is a lie!" she cried.

I hastened to make amends. "Please tell me your name," I repeated. The queen was watching closely.

"Yusra. I am called Yusra." The words came out in the barest of whispers.

Yusra. Her name means "ease after hardship." I turned to the queen.

"Her name is Yusra," I said. "She says her father is captain of the ship we sank."

"Was captain," Queen Joanna replied. "I know he was among those who were killed." She looked toward Yusra, her eyes full of compassion. "Poor child. Tell her she will be taken care of, Matthew."

"You are in no danger here," I said, trying to make my voice gentle and calming, the way I would have spoken to my little goat if she had been upset. Indeed, this girl looked more fragile and frightened than any small beast I had ever seen. A thought struck me then. "Do you know who this lady is?"

"No," she said.

"She is a great queen. She was queen of Sicily and is sister to the king of England himself."

"She is a queen?" The girl wiped quickly at her eyes with the back of one hand. "Ask her, then . . . Ask her to let me see my father."

"Your father . . ." I stumbled over the words, then summoned up the courage to speak them. Truly, I dreaded the effect they would have on this small creature. "Your father is dead. I'm sorry." I reached out a hand to her, but she shrank back.

"Dead? That cannot be!" she gasped.

"It is true. I'm sorry," I stammered again. What else could I say?

"It's not true," she cried. "It's not true!" Her face suddenly paled. "And my mother?" Her voice was so low now I could hardly hear her.

"Your mother? She was on the ship as well?" My

heart took a leaden plunge downward.

She nodded. She was holding herself as still as if she had turned to stone. "My father always took us on his voyages."

I looked to the queen. "Her mother, Your Grace. Her mother was on board as well."

"There was no other woman among the survivors." The queen shook her head slowly. "The poor creature has lost both her father and her mother and now she's alone amongst strangers. I know something of what that feels like—I must do what I can for her." She looked toward Father Aimar as if seeking help, but he was staring at Yusra, face grim.

Yusra knew by the tone of the queen's voice what she had said. She collapsed, her face buried in the pillows.

I stood there, feeling as awkward and as sorry for anyone as I have ever felt in my life. There was a long moment of silence, and then the queen spoke.

"Go, Matthew. I thank you for helping me with her, but I think you have done all you can now." She reached out a hand to stroke the girl's head, but Yusra flinched away from her touch. The queen dropped her hand and sighed. "I will call for you again, Matthew. I think we will have need of you to help with this poor child. But go now," she repeated.

I made my obeisance and backed away.

I cannot put the remembrance of that small, huddled figure out of my mind. What is to become of her? I cannot imagine.

Later again . . .

We sailed into the harbor at Acre late this afternoon. It is a well-protected harbor, close up against
the walls of the city. We dropped sails and the oarsmen took us in. The sea was calm, but small waves
raced along the base of the walls like fingers of foam
determined to find their way in. We could see
figures moving around the ramparts. They seemed
to have no fear of being fired upon, which I found
strange. They were Saracens, after all, and the
Christian army surrounds the city.

As I drank in the sights and the salty, kelpy smell
of the sea, I heard the Muslim call to prayer begin.
I have heard this many times in Sicily and never,
truth to tell, paid much attention to it, but somehow here, on the shores of this strange land, it
sounded new and different to me. Oddly
compelling. The call seemed to have the same effect
on everyone aboard the ship. Gradually a strange
silence fell. I could hear naught but the creaking
and plashing of oars. Then, from the hills far inland,
an answering echo to the prayer song rang out. I
turned to face the shore itself. The Christian army
was camped around the walls of the city for as far as
I could see. Figures bustled about there as well.
Behind our army the ground swelled into high hills
and peaks. It was there, I heard, that the camp of
Salah-ud-Din lay, and it was from there that the
echoing call to prayer came. I stared at those hills,
imagining the size and force of that army. For the
first time I truly realized the plight of the Christian
crusaders. We, the besiegers of Acre, are besieged

ourselves and surrounded at every point except for the coast.

As the last notes of the Muslim call to prayer were dying, a huge commotion broke out on shore. Suddenly there was noise and shouting everywhere. Trumpets blared, mingled with clarions and flutes. People poured down to the harbor where our ships were docking. They sang and they danced and they threw garlands and nosegays of flowers. Then King Richard appeared on deck in the most resplendent attire I have seen yet, and I thought the people would go mad with cheering. He strode on shore, followed closely by Queen Berengaria and Queen Joanna. Queen Berengaria looked frightened. Behind them trailed Yusra, looking even more frightened. Father Aimar had his hand on her shoulder. I suppose it was to guide her, but I wonder whether it might also have been there to keep her from running away—although where they expected her to run to I cannot imagine.

All during the time we unloaded the ships and set up camp the festivities increased. Indeed, they are still going on even as I write this. I must stop now though and try to sleep. I have been given a small tent not too far from the king's own pavilion. Now that we are here and settled, I will most likely be called to work tomorrow and I must be fresh and alert.

But how am I supposed to sleep with all this excitement? I cannot wait to see what the morrow will bring.

The ninth day of June

Where to begin? Where I left off last night, I suppose, but there is so much to tell my hand is cramping at the very thought of it. I must write it down, however. What I have seen today I must not forget.

I was called by one of King Richard's men just as the dawn was breaking. I had not slept a wink, of course. I do not think the king had slept either, as he was dressed just as I had seen him yesterday and had a stubble of beard on his chin. Very unusual this was for him. He is always most meticulous in his habits. Nonetheless, he was brighter and more awake than I. To my horror I even yawned as I knelt to greet him, but I think I covered it up well enough with a cough.

The tent was filled with people. I recognized many of the nobles of Ôutremer. They looked decidedly unhappy. Then I saw the king's senior scribe, Bertrand. I have seen him before, of course, but he is much more grand than I and did not deign to acknowledge my existence. He was seated at a plank that served as a table and was busily writing.

"I am having a notice written," the king thundered. He looked annoyed. "A proclamation. It seems our good King Philip is offering three gold bezants to any man who will follow him. I distrust his motives and do not intend to let him build up a force larger than my own." He gestured to me. "You will help write it. I need all the copies we can make as quickly as possible."

I pulled out my quills and ink and made ready.

There was no room at the table where Bertrand worked, and I would not have dared to join him in any case, but I spied a trunk nearby him. I made room for myself on it and spread out a parchment. What joy it is to write on finely cured parchment instead of smelly, rough skins!

"Write!" the king commanded, and I did. "'The king of England will pay *four* gold bezants to any knight of any nationality who would take service under his banner.' Make as many copies as you can, in all the languages you boasted you could." He glared at me from under bushy golden eyebrows. I dropped my eyes, gulped for air, became immediately busy and promptly blotted a parchment. Thanks be to heaven he didn't see, but turned to the other men who waited on him.

"Two years!" His voice filled the tent. "Two years this impossible stalemate has lasted." He strode back and forth from one side of the pavilion to the other, slapping at his thigh with a leather gauntlet. He was glowering at the men so hard that he nearly ran me down. I ducked just in time as he veered off. A servant bearing wine was not quite so fortunate. The king walked right into him and the wine cascaded onto the floor. The poor fellow lost his wits entirely and bolted for the door. Luckily for him the king was so overwrought he didn't notice that upset either.

"God's legs—most of the time they have not even been fighting! Worse, it seems the two camps have been consorting back and forth! Christian soldiers have taken part in Muslim celebrations and

Muslims have walked freely amongst us. I have seen them with my own eyes. Philip has not done a thing since he arrived." He slapped even harder at his leg. "Well, I am here now," he bellowed, "and the Saracens will learn to tremble at the roar of this lion!" He looked back to me.

"When the notices are ready you will post them everywhere you can," he said. He frowned at me as if I were personally responsible for the whole situation. "We will spread the word. The king of England pays better than the king of France to any knight of any nationality who would take service under my banner."

"Yes, Sire," I said.

I wrote as many notices as I had parchments for, collected up the others, went out to post them around the camp and immediately fell into an adventure. But I can write no longer tonight. I will have to continue tomorrow.

The tenth day of June

The camp is full beyond belief. I had thought Messina crowded when the crusading armies poured in upon us, but that was nothing compared to what exists here. Our camp is stretched in a narrow band around the city, squashed between the two Muslim forces. Salah-ud-Din's army presses down on us from the hills, and the garrison in the city keeps us at bay on the other side. There are men, and women also, packed in here from France, England, Germany, Italy and scores of other places. The whole world has come on crusade to Acre, it seems.

And there are horses, goats, cows and other strange animals called camels. These are gawky, awkward, mean-spirited beasts that spit and bite, but they are invaluable in this arid land, I am told. They can carry enormous packs and go for days without water.

To add to all the confusion siege engines are being constructed in every available space. Piles of baggage and supplies are lying around and more tents have sprung up than I have ever seen before in one place. The noise and smell beggar description. I have to step very carefully for every piece of land is covered with garbage or filth. Flies are everywhere. And it is hot! I am used to heat, but this is beyond anything I have ever felt. The sea breeze does not reach into the camp itself, and the air hangs heavy and fetid over everyone and everything. My hands are so wet with sweat at this very moment that I can hardly write, and the tunic I wear is soaked and sticking to my back. My hair drips into my eyes.

King Richard was right about the fraternization between the two camps. I saw many Saracens wandering freely about. In one tent at the edge of the camp I even saw a Christian knight and a Muslim warrior, both armed to the teeth with swords and daggers, sitting opposite each other, laughing and playing chess!

It was as I was watching them that my adventure happened.

I was loitering by the tent, trying to fathom how the game was played, when I suddenly heard a shout. At the same time I saw a horse bearing down upon me. It was a magnificent black stallion, but it was being ridden mercilessly. The animal's eyes were rolled back in its head as if it were trying to see what manner of demon was on its back. Its teeth were bared and its head was forced back by the hands yanking on the reins. Foam flecked its mouth, and the beast neighed in terror as it galloped toward me.

"Stop him!" The shout was in Arabic and came from somewhere behind me. "Stop that thief! That's my horse!"

I didn't have time to think. As the horse thundered toward me, instead of leaping aside I stepped deliberately into its path. I do not know what possessed me to do that. By all rights I should have been mown down and killed instantly. Instead, the stallion braced its forelegs in mid-stride and came to a jarring halt barely a cart's length away from me. The rider, taken by surprise, sailed over the animal's head and landed in a heap, but he was on his feet in an instant and ran off. I grabbed the dangling bridle of the horse and tried to calm the animal. Again, I should have been kicked to death by the flying hooves, but instead the beast gave an enormous shudder and let me bring it under control.

At that moment a Muslim warrior raced up. He tore the bridle out of my hands, leaped up on the horse's back and, before I could say anything, spurred the animal off in pursuit of the thief. I was left standing there empty-handed and dumbfounded.

Now that I write this account, it doesn't seem like such an adventure. In fact, I am beginning to get angry. Not one word of thanks did I get for risking my life. Barely a glance did the warrior give me. I might have been the lowliest of slaves for all the notice he took of me.

Still, the incident has given me an idea. If Muslim nobles and warriors can make so free with our camp, why should I not visit theirs? King Richard is so set on war, this peaceful state of commingling might not last much longer. I should go now or I might lose my chance altogether.

And perhaps I might see that warrior again. I wouldn't mind letting him know what I think of him.

The horse was a splendid animal though. I am pleased that I saved him from that thief.

The eleventh day of June

By noon today the king had finished with me and let me go.

"I will not need you again today, boy," he said.

I left his tent and headed back to my own. There I stashed my quills and inkhorn and ate a quick meal of bread and cheese. I quaffed a horn of ale too, not so much from thirst as from a need for courage. For I had decided to steal out to see the Muslim camp for myself. In spite of my brave words yesterday, I was afraid this was not a wise decision. In fact, I knew for certain it was not a wise decision, but I had made up my mind to do it and do it I would.

I had to be a little devious however. The crusaders are beginning to prepare for war and I was not entirely certain that I would be allowed to leave. To be safe, I made my way through the bushes until I was out of sight of the soldiers who guard the perimeters of the camp.

The sun was past its zenith and the Muslim afternoon call to prayer was just beginning as I set my feet on the path that led into the hills. It took me much longer than I thought to reach the Muslim camp. The path became steeper and steeper, and I labored to catch my breath. I had to stop more and more often to rest and relieve the ache in my foot. I began to think the whole venture a huge mistake, but my curiosity has always led me around by the nose and this time was no exception.

I thought it prudent to exercise the same caution entering the Muslim camp as I had leaving the Christian camp, so when I saw the fires of their guards, I avoided them. Then I made my way closer and closer to the tents and pavilions themselves. They seemed much more grand than our own— even grander than the king's. They shimmered in the late afternoon sunlight as if made of silk, and pennants and streamers flew from every one. I could see women tending fires around them. They all wore scarves covering their heads, as did the Muslim women of Sicily. Children ran around like chickens. The air was fresher here in the hills, and I noticed far fewer insects. Salah-ud-Din certainly had by far the better campsite.

There was the same bustle and flurry of activity in this camp as in my own, but I was becoming uncomfortably aware that I could see no other Christians. A few people cast suspicious looks toward me. I was beginning to feel ill at ease and very much afraid that I had made a foolhardy decision in going there when a voice suddenly hissed in my ear.

"What are you doing here, Christian boy? The time for friendliness between our camps is past, now that your English king is come and preaching war. Are you spying on us?"

I felt a hand grab my arm, then my other arm was seized as well. Before I realized what was happening, I found myself being dragged through the bushes into a small clearing.

I collected my wits and began to protest, but my words were cut off by a blow to my back that knocked all the breath out of my body. I fell face forward in the dust and then a vicious kick in the ribs knocked the breath out of me again. In spite of myself I cried out in pain. I scrambled to my knees and knelt there, trying to breathe, but another kick, this time to my face, sent me rolling. I ended up on my back with my eyes tight shut and my arms crossed in front of my face for protection. God in heaven, I remember thinking, what have I got myself into? What have I done?

The blows ceased for a moment and I fought for the strength to speak, to explain myself before they began again.

"I just wanted to visit . . . to see your camp . . ." My lungs burned with the effort. "I am no spy!"

"A Christian who speaks Arabic that well—you must be one!" said the voice.

I saw then that there were two assailants. One of them drew back his arm, ready to strike me again.

"I swear I am not," I cried.

Then the other laughed. "How could he be?" he sneered. "Look at his foot. He is just a helpless cripple."

"He was skulking around our camp," the first one said. He drew a dagger from his belt and stepped forward. I felt a cold chill catch hold of my heart as he pressed the tip of it to my throat. I stopped breathing. "Spy or not, he has no business here now. Should we kill him ourselves or take him to the guards?"

"Why bother the guards with such an insignificant nuisance?" the other answered.

I couldn't believe what I was hearing. Surely they were just trying to frighten me. I held myself as still as if I had been turned to stone and prayed harder than I have ever prayed in my life.

Just then a voice rang out. "Leave him!" Another figure stepped into the clearing. The glint of a scimitar reflected the sun's last rays. My tormentors stared for a moment. Then one whispered something I could not hear to the other and, to my surprise and immense relief, they ran off like a pair of frightened hounds.

The figure strode into full view and stood before me. His eyes widened.

"You!" he said. "You are the boy who rescued my beloved Muharib for me."

"Muharib?" I stuttered. My head was swimming.

"My horse. You stopped that thief from taking off with him."

In that instant I recognized him. He was not a

grown man as I had thought. In fact, he was probably not much older than I. I struggled to gather my wits about me. There was much I wanted to say to him.

"I was going to go back to your camp to search for you and apologize. I treated you badly—I am sorry. I was in such haste to capture that wretch who had dared to steal Muharib that I did not thank you. Or reward you."

My ears pricked up at the mention of reward, and my resentment toward him began to lessen. After all, he had probably just saved my life.

"Those knaves will be caught and punished," he said. "You may be certain of it. When I heard them in here I knew they were up to no good— they have caused trouble in the camp before. But that they should attack you . . . you who showed such bravery yesterday . . . I must apologize."

I finally collected myself enough to speak, but he forestalled me.

"And to make such improper remarks about your affliction. That is against the teaching of Islam. It is unforgivable," he said.

I made an effort to stand. A sudden pain knifed through my head and I staggered. The Muslim boy caught me.

"But you are hurt," he said. "Come with me. My tent is nearby. I will have your wounds tended to. My name is Rashid," he added.

"I am Matthew," I managed to say in return. I clutched onto him for support. Only then did I realize blood was flowing down my face from my nose.

(It is broken, by the way, and is paining me beyond belief as I write this. It will most certainly heal crooked. Perhaps that is not such a bad thing though. Perhaps it will give me a more dangerous look.)

The words blur before my eyes. I must sleep. I will try to finish my story tomorrow. There is still much to tell, but I cannot write more now.

The twelfth day of June

As I wrote this date down on my parchment I remembered that today is the day of my birth. I have lived in this world for sixteen years. I suppose I am a man now. But a very sore and wounded man. I swear there is not a bone in my body that does not ache. My nose is swollen to the size of a turnip. It took the greatest of efforts to report to the king's tent for my work this morning. Luckily he is preoccupied these days and after one quick question about my face he did not mention it further.

"I took a fall, Sire," I said. A feeble explanation, but he was not in the mood to concern himself with it. It has been an arduous day and I wish for nothing more than to sink into sleep, but I will finish my tale first. It is truly amazing how important the writing of this journal has become to me.

I allowed Rashid to lead me through the trees to a large tent. There were sentries posted outside it, but he spoke a few words to them and they drew back to let us enter. As he held open the flap and motioned me to go in, I could not help but draw in my breath with amazement.

The interior was lit by bowls of aromatic oils with

burning wicks floating in them. The walls were covered with shimmering silken hangings in the richest colors. The earthen floor was soft with deep, lush carpets. Near the back pillows lay in inviting mounds.

"Sit," Rashid commanded.

I did as I was bade. Rashid clapped his hands and one of the sentries appeared. He gave an order, then a maid arrived with a basin of water. She must have been a slave, as she wore no head covering. She would have bathed my face, but her ministrations made me feel awkward and uncomfortable. "I would do it myself," I said, hoping I did not sound ungracious.

"As you wish," Rashid answered. He motioned to the girl to leave.

Thanks be to God, the bleeding from my nose stopped. I washed and tidied myself as best as I could, desperately trying not to soil the pillows or rugs upon which I sat. How different this tent was from my own rough shelter!

How different, indeed. As I composed myself and looked around I was astonished to see a chest with fine parchment scrolls and even books lying on it. In our camp only the king and the priests have such things.

"Now," Rashid said, "something to give you back your strength." He held out a bowl of fruit to me. I took a fig.

"Thank you," I said. I peeled the skin back and bit into the flesh. It was cool and sweet and washed the taste of blood away.

"It is I who should thank you," Rashid answered. "I could not have borne it if I had lost Muharib."

"You have more than repaid me," I said. "If you had not appeared when you did tonight, I do not think I would have left here alive."

Perhaps I should not have been so gracious as there was then no more talk of reward.

"What were you doing here?" he asked.

"I just wanted to see your camp. I was not spying," I added quickly.

"I do not think you were," he said. "But you are not a warrior?"

"No," I answered. "I am a scribe. I am scribe to King Richard himself." I knew that he had meant no insult, but he had glanced at my foot in spite of himself when he had asked that question and my pride was pricked.

"A scribe!" he cried, and sat bolt upright. "Truly, I knew you were a man of importance! That is the most honorable of professions. We hold scribes in the highest regard."

I cannot quite describe the feeling that came over me then. It was the first time in my life that anyone had ever suggested I was a person of any worth. I almost felt as if my soul were growing larger within my body. I know I sat taller. I am still sitting taller, even though at this moment I am racked with pain and exhaustion.

"But you should go back to your own camp now," Rashid said then.

I looked at him, startled. Was he angry after all?

"It is ungracious of me, I know," he added

quickly, "but for your own safety I must urge you to leave." He took a fig himself and bit into it, then threw it aside as if it tasted bitter. "It is true that we have visited back and forth between camps often in the past two years," he said, "but now with the arrival of your English king, things are different. Feelings are running high. I would not be welcome in your camp anymore and, I am afraid, as you have found out, you are not welcome here."

"You are right," I said. "I should not have come."

"But I am glad you did," Rashid said. He rose to his feet. I rose as well.

We stared at each other for a long, awkward moment. It seemed to me, and to him as well, I think, that there should have been something else to say, but neither of us could imagine what it was. After all, we were supposed to be enemies. We would probably be at war with each other within weeks, possibly days. And yet, as I looked at him, I could not help feeling that if circumstances had been different this boy might have been the first real friend I had ever had in my life.

Finally he spoke.

"I will have my sentry escort you safely to the edge of our camp," he said.

"Thank you," I answered.

"Assalamu alaikum," he added quietly. "The peace be on you."

"God be with you," I replied.

There was nothing else to say.

It was almost morning and the first Muslim call

to prayer of the day was just breaking the dark still-
ness of the night when I finally stumbled back here
into my tent, my foot throbbing and my head swimming with the pain of my broken nose.

Rashid. "The rightly guided one," his name
means. He is not much older than I, but he is obviously a person of great importance.

And he believes me to be a person of importance
too.

The thirteenth day of June

I saw Yusra this morning, but could not speak to
her. Queen Joanna keeps her close by and has not
called for me again. I wonder how things are faring
with her. She does not look happy.

The smell of battle is in the air. Men are nervous
and so tightly strung that fights break out over the
least disagreement. King Richard's castle, Mategriffon, is being reassembled and will be used as a
siege tower when we attack. It is even taller than the
city walls and has enormous wheels on it now so
that it can be pushed close up to the walls when the
time comes. Inside, there is a staircase leading up to
the higher levels. There are platforms on every stage
from whence our archers and crossbowmen can
shoot, and on the top level a drawbridge has been
built that can be lowered to span the gap between
the castle itself and the wall, over which a storming
party can launch an attack. The whole structure is
covered with skins of cattle. When the battle starts
they will be drenched with water so that the flaming
Greek fire the Saracens hurl at us will not set it

ablaze. If there is not enough water we will soak it in vinegar and urine.

This Greek fire is fearsome. I had never seen it before in Sicily. The Christian armies have discovered the secret of it, and I pestered Rigord until he agreed to allow me to watch as our men loaded one of the catapults with some early this morning before dawn. It looks to be no more than a pottery container filled with some kind of sour juice, but in fact the fluid is made of an oil that bursts into flame easily and burns for a long time. While our soldiers loaded, the Saracens began to bombard us with the same material—and I began to think I had made a mistake in wanting to be there. Flaming balls arced through the sky toward us, trailing burning tails the length of a long sword. They gave such a great light that our whole camp was as bright as day. The noise they made was thunderous, such as I imagine a dragon or some other terrible beast would make flying through the air. When they landed, the containers burst and the flames spread everywhere. The mixture is so powerful that water will not put it out.

I think I have seen enough of it at such close quarters now and will not pester Rigord about it again.

As usual I listen to more than I am supposed to, and I have found out that King Richard intends to start the attack as soon as possible. Other great siege engines are being assembled, but these are mostly stone-throwing mangonels. They bear noble names, and already The Cat, God's Own Sling and The Evil Neighbor (Philip's best mangonel) are hurling great rocks at the city walls. King Richard is like a man possessed. He walks among the troops, encouraging them and doing everything he can to lift their spirits.

King Philip is a disaster as a leader. He seems to dislike the whole business of war and so far has done little but sit gloomily in his tent, soaking the atmosphere around him with dejection. His mood has spread to the whole camp, but King Richard is determined to change that.

The Saracens no longer visit us. I wonder where Rashid is and what he is doing.

The fourteenth day of June

King Richard attacked the city at dawn this morning! I was awoken by the sound of trumpets just as the sun was rising. I knew at once what must be happening. I leaped up off my pallet and scrambled outside. There is a small knoll behind my tent and I made for that so as to see what was going on. My heart began to pound as I saw King Richard's and King Philip's armies assembling on the outskirts of the city.

I could hear nothing but men shouting orders, horses bellowing and curses heating up the air as the soldiers jostled for position. To me it seemed like total chaos, but to my amazement the whole mess gradually sorted itself out and the siege engines began to bombard the city with flaming missiles and stones.

Then, as I watched, I saw the parapets of the city walls suddenly come alive with soldiers. At that exact moment the crusading armies attacked. They thundered toward the walls. Trumpets blared and pennants flew. My heart began to beat so hard I thought it would shake me to pieces. From where I stood I had an excellent view of everything, and for the first time in my life I found myself longing to be in the battle. To be a man, amongst other men, who could fight! I felt stirrings within such as I have never felt before, but there was nothing for me to do but watch. How useless I am!

Then the sky turned black with arrows. They rained down upon our attacking crusaders. I heard screams. Men fell, horses crashed to the ground. I squinted, desperately trying to keep King Richard's banner in sight, and stopped breathing when I saw it plunge to the ground. In a flash it was overtrampled and lost to view. I didn't draw breath again until I saw the king's golden hair flaming in the sunlight. He was at the very forefront of his men, his sword thrusting and cutting so quickly it was just a blur.

I was watching the assault on the city so intently that I was shocked by a sudden clamor of wailing horns and wild war cries. Salah-ud-Din's forces streamed down from the mountains behind us and charged into the rear of our army, turning the battle into churning turmoil. The brilliant colors of the Muslim warriors flashed in and out amongst the shining mail of the crusaders. Swords slashed and clanged. I did not see how anyone could possibly know what was happening. Trumpets rang out again and to my horror I saw our soldiers begin to fall back, still fighting. At the camp's edge, Salah-ud-Din's army pulled up. I saw a richly robed figure on a white stallion at the head of the Saracens and knew this had to be the sultan himself. He sat for a long moment, triumphant, then turned and galloped his army away, back into the hills.

Was Rashid with them? He must have been. He most certainly would not have been as useless as I.

The fifteenth day of June

Now we suffer. Our men lie strewn on the ground between us and the city walls. We cannot go out to them. Anyone who tries is picked off by the arrows of the defenders on the walls. Most of the men out there are dead, but some are still alive. We can hear their cries. I pace up and down along the edge of the campsite. I cannot take my eyes off them. I want to stop my ears against the sound of their calls for help and their moans, but I cannot. I have to listen. To look.

I cannot believe that yesterday I was so carried away with the bloodlust of battle that I wanted to be a part of it. Today all I feel is sick.

The sun is full up now and the heat has brought out the flies. They cluster on the bodies and fill the air around me. I cannot breathe without inhaling the tiny insects. The smell from the battlefield is beginning to waft over us, overpowering all other stinks. The vultures are feasting. It is unbearable.

Our camp is silent. We are prepared for an attack, but the Muslim forces in the hills are silent too. Only the calls to prayer ring out at their regular, appointed times. Our priests cover their ears when they hear them.

The sixteenth day of June

The Muslim army has not attacked. Our camp is still at the ready, but our men are managing to retrieve the bodies of our soldiers. The Muslim bowmen stand on the parapets and watch, but are no longer shooting at them. I do not believe any of the wounded have survived though. It is too late for them.

Late yesterday afternoon I was summoned to King Richard's pavilion. Bertrand, his senior scribe, is ill. The king himself does not look well, but perhaps it is only the aftermath of the battle. In any case he was most brusque with me.

"Bertrand cannot work," he said. "You will take over his duties until he is fit again."

Before I had time to realize just what he meant, he threw a parchment to me and motioned me over to Bertrand's table.

"I will dictate to you. You will write an account of the battle. It is imperative everything that happens here be written down. There must be a record kept of it. A truthful account." He broke off as if a thought had just occurred to him, and stared at me.

"Where were you, boy, during the battle?"

I flushed so deeply my skin burned.

"I watched, Sire. From a hill." My shame at uttering these words was so great that they came out almost in a whisper. I braced myself to hear words of contempt, but to my surprise the king nodded as if satisfied.

"Good. Then you will be able to write as well of what the battle looked like to an observer. When one is in the midst of the fighting, one cannot always tell what is going on. Your own account will be most useful. Add it to mine."

In shock I scrambled to get my writing implements in order.

"God's legs, boy, are you not ready yet?" the king growled.

"I am, Sire," I replied, although I wasn't quite. He began to dictate and I raced to keep up with his words. Then, when he was finished, he stood over me while I added the account of the battle as I had seen it. When I had finished he grunted.

"You write well, boy," he said.

I flushed again, but he nodded to the tent door. "Out with you now," he ordered.

I am sitting here, scribbling in my own journal, but my mind is stirring with new thoughts. Could it be that I am useful after all? I am the only scribe in King Richard's camp now. If I do not record the account of what happens, it will not be written down—at least not by us. I suppose there is a scribe recording it all in King Philip's camp. I wonder how he views what has happened. Does he write as glowingly of his king as I do of mine? If he does, I do not believe it would be the truth, as I feel King Philip is cowardly and evasive. And yet King Philip's scribe might believe him to be as valiant as I believe my king to be. His scribe might believe my king to be the weaker and write that.

Yet another thought. What will the Saracen account of the battle be? Different again, I would wager. Three accounts of the same battle. All must be different and yet each of us would believe our own account to be the true one and those who read our accounts will believe that too.

But do I really believe mine to be absolutely true? In my account I did not include seeing Salah-ud-Din sitting triumphantly on his horse, gloating over the scene of battle—I did not wish to offend my king. But by leaving this out, was I not altering the account of what happened just as surely as if I had lied?

The seventeenth day of June

I have been burning with curiosity to know how my little maid from the sea has been faring and today, finally, I was summoned to Queen Joanna's pavilion. The king would not give me leave to go until I had finished my work with him, however. Bertrand is even more ill and the king's doctors hold out little hope for him. King Richard himself is pale and sweating. I fear he also has the fever. This heat is agony to all of us, but especially so to him. It was so hot inside his pavilion that I almost swooned myself. My head was aching and swimming by the time I left. Outside it is a little better, but the flies are a torment from hell. The smell of the camp is indescribable.

As soon as I had finished and the king had dismissed me I made my way to Queen Joanna's tent. When I reached it I was shown in immediately. The queen was pacing back and forth. Yusra huddled on a pillow, shoulders hunched and arms wrapped tightly around herself as if for safety. Her eyes were fixed on the ground. Her hair fell down around her face, half obscuring it.

"I can do nothing with this child, Matthew, and I am losing patience," the queen said. She sounded exasperated. "She does not weep anymore, but she will not respond to me, no matter how kindly I treat her. Will you try again?"

I dropped to one knee and made obeisance to her awkwardly. As usual, my foot got in the way.

"I will, Your Grace," I answered. Then I knelt down completely so that I would be at the girl's level.

"Yusra," I said in my best goat-calming voice, "the queen is trying to help you. We know how you must feel. We are truly sorry for you. What can we do?"

"Nothing." Her eyes stayed fixed on the rug beneath her feet. "My parents are dead. I am a prisoner. There is nothing you can do."

"You are not a prisoner," I said.

At that she looked up. "I'm not?"

"No, of course not," I repeated. "The king of England does not take children prisoner."

She straightened. "Then tell him to let me go. Tell him to send me back to my own people."

I looked at the queen. "She wishes to be returned to her own people," I said.

The queen spread her hands helplessly. "Impossible. We are at war now. She must stay with us, but we will treat her well. Tell her that."

I translated as best I could. Yusra's face hardened and her mouth set into a stubborn line.

"I will never be happy here. I will die first."

I looked at the queen. She had not understood the words, but she seemed to understand Yusra's tone all too well. She shook her head in annoyance and motioned me to leave.

There must be some way to get through to that girl. I am going to keep on trying if the queen will let me. I feel she is my responsibility. After all, it was I who rescued her.

She is just a child, I know, but she would probably be quite a pretty one if she ever smiled.

The nineteenth day of June

Bertrand has died. The king is now deathly ill as well. What will happen to us if King Richard dies?

The twentieth day of June

A most amazing occurrence, and one that will take some time telling. Shortly after the Muslim call to prayer this morning and after our own priests had said mass, horns sounded at the outskirts of our camp. Everyone was immediately galvanized. Was this the attack by Salah-ud-Din's forces that we had been waiting for? While the soldiers rallied, the ordinary people who have come on crusade with us began to pour out of their tents, screaming and running in all directions. Thanks be it wasn't an assault or they would have been easily massacred. It sometimes seems to me that people have less sense than goats.

In any case it was a small party of Muslim warriors under a flag of truce. Truly they were brave men, for they rode confidently and without hesitation into our camp. They were of obvious importance. They were richly robed and carried themselves with the bearing of kings. No fewer than four horsemen held their brightly colored standards.

From the vantage point of my tent I watched them approach. After the initial shock, once they realized there was no danger, people began filtering back. The first, of course, were the children. Raga-muffins of all sizes were soon parading alongside the Muslim party. They hooted and called out, but the warriors paid them no attention. One small urchin even went so far as to throw a stone, but an older child scolded him and called out an apology.

It was then I saw Rashid riding behind and to the right of the leader. He was mounted on his horse, Muharib, and sat straight and tall in his saddle, his eyes focused straight ahead. He was garbed in the vibrant colors of a Muslim warrior and wore a scarlet turban on his head. If he was aware of the child rabble running alongside them he gave no indication. I was astonished. I had not really expected to see him again, certainly not in this guise.

The party approached the tent. Rigord stepped forward and challenged them.

"What wish you, my lords?" he asked, but his tone was respectful.

"We bear gifts from Salah-ud-Din to your king. Our sultan has heard that your leader is ill. We bring ice from the mountains to help cool his fever, and fruits to fortify him against the illness."

I could not believe my ears. We were at war!

Salah-ud-Din had just defeated us in a terrible battle. Now he was sending succor to our king? I had to know more of this. And Rashid, what was he doing with this party? Who was he? I slipped from my tent and fell in behind the Muslim warriors. I hung back until Rigord had secured permission for them to enter, then, as they were dismounting, I followed. Rigord started to restrain me, but I spoke sharply to him.

"The king will have need of me," I said in the best semblance of the king's own tone that I could manage. Luckily Rigord couldn't see the shaking that was going on inside me. He hesitated, then stood back to let me pass.

It was a delicious moment. For the first time in my life I gave an order. And it was obeyed! This business of being the only scribe is beginning to suit me.

I followed the Muslim warriors into the pavilion. The smell of sickness hit us as soon as the tent flap closed behind us. I had been in there this morning, asking futilely if the king had need of my services. It had been bad then, but was worse now. I had even heard that Richard's hair and nails had begun to fall out.

The king sat propped up on pillows. His face was deathly white and dripping with sweat. His glorious golden hair hung in limp, dark strands around his shoulders. Behind him stood his most trusted lieutenant, Mercadier, and two servants. Mercadier's hand was upon his dagger as he frowned at the Muslim party. King Richard's arm shook as he raised it in greeting. He was deathly ill. But there was still about him an air of majesty that lesser men such as King Philip could never achieve. He saw me and motioned me closer. I could feel myself swelling almost to the bursting point with importance. I hoped Rigord was watching.

"You will translate for me, Matthew," he said. The effort of speaking seemed to exhaust him, but he rallied and turned toward the Muslim delegation.

"You are well come, my lords," he said. I translated the words.

The leader returned the greeting.

"Peace be with you," he said. "The blessings of God be upon you. The great sultan, Al-Malik al-Nasir Salah-ud-Din Yusuf ibn Ayyud, has sent these gifts with the hope they might help you." He motioned a man forward. The man crouched before the king, bearing a straw-covered bundle that was dripping water. I stared at Rashid, but he seemed not to notice I was there.

"Ice, Your Majesty, to soothe your fever," the Muslim leader went on. He motioned another man forward. This one bore a large basket. "And the freshest fruits from our orchards. You westerners do not eat sufficiently of this bounty. Their goodness drives away all sickness."

I was translating as fast as I could.

"I thank you," King Richard replied. He sank back onto his cushions. "I would rise to give you proper homage but I cannot . . ."

I was so surprised that for a moment I was at a

loss for words. King Richard, apologizing to a Muslim! He waved an impatient hand at me and I made haste to convey his words.

At that point the leader of the Muslim party interrupted me.

"I speak French, my lord," he said. "We can converse in that language if you wish, without need of a translator."

The king looked relieved. I was annoyed.

"Pray be seated then," King Richard said, indicating the pillows strewn around his tent. "I would converse with you. You may go, Matthew," he added.

"God's legs," I muttered resentfully as I took myself out. "Just when things were getting interesting." Again I tried to catch Rashid's eye, but he would not look at me.

Rigord smirked as I limped away. I didn't feel quite so important anymore.

Later . . .

I had to stop writing because the king sent for me. Late though it is he decided he had to dictate a reply thanking the sultan for his gifts. He seemed somewhat refreshed and less feverish, so the ice and fruit must have done him good. It is almost time for the Muslim morning call to prayer, but I will write until I finish this, even if I do not sleep at all. I am in such a state that I probably will not, in any case.

I had hardly taken more than a few steps away from the king's tent, still resentful at being dismissed, before I heard someone on the path behind me. I swung around, on the alert.

"Stay," a low voice said in Arabic. "It is I, Rashid. I wanted to speak further with you. I begged leave of my uncle to follow you."

I collected my wits as quickly as I could. "Your uncle?"

"My uncle is the one who speaks with your king now. He is one of our great sultan's most trusted advisors."

No wonder those rogues had been afraid of Rashid. He comes from a powerful family.

"How fares your nose?" Rashid asked.

I laughed. "A little crooked, as you can see, and still mightily swollen, but it pains me less now. It was kind of your sultan to send such gifts to my king," I added. "Usually men at war do not treat each other with such consideration."

"Our sultan is a courteous man of infinite mercy and compassion. He would not let a fellow man suffer needlessly," he said.

I could not hold my tongue at that, no matter how grateful I was to Rashid for saving me.

"Your sultan has the reputation of being among the fiercest of warriors. What I have seen here bears that reputation out."

"And so he is. In war you must kill or be killed." He stopped and looked at me. His eyes narrowed. "You must know, my friend, that our sultan is only defending land that is rightfully ours. Why should you come from the west and try to take it from us?

Why should any of you be here at all? This is not your land."

"Your sultan took Jerusalem from us." I was becoming angry in spite of myself. "It was a Christian city. A holy city!"

"It is also a holy city to all of Islam. You Christians took it first from us. And when *you* took Jerusalem your Christian crusaders massacred every Muslim man, woman and child in the city. Not in the heat of battle, but after you had won. You even massacred the Jews, people of the Book such as you are yourselves. When our sultan retook the city he spared every Christian in it. He did not kill one. The Christians live there even now in peace and harmony with Jews and Muslims alike. Salah-ud-Din is a merciful conqueror."

I stared at him. This was not the history I had heard.

Rashid shook his head. He seemed to make an effort to control himself. Then he went on in a calmer voice.

"We should not be enemies, the people of Islam and yourselves. You are people of the Book, you and the Jews as well. The Book that tells of the old prophets we all share, Muslims, Jews and Christians alike. It is unfortunate that you blaspheme and have gone astray, but we worship the same God. I enjoyed conversing with your priests in the days before your English king came."

"The Book?" I managed to get out. In truth, I was so confounded by what he had said that I could not make sense of it. I remembered the books and scrolls I had seen in his tent. "You have read our Bible?" No one I knew had read this most holy of Christian books, only the priests. I doubted that even the king owned such a thing.

"No, I have not read your Bible. I read the Qur'an, the divine revelation given to our prophet, Muhammad, God's peace and blessing be on him, but it tells of the history that we have in common. It was the angel Gabriel who gave God's holy revelation to our prophet, Muhammad, God's peace and blessing be on him. The same angel who brought God's message to you Christians."

At that moment a voice rang out. "Rashid! Come!"

"My uncle calls. I must go," Rashid said. "We should talk more, Matthew. Perhaps some day we will be able to. Perhaps . . ."

His uncle called again. He held out his hand.

"Assalamu alaikum," he said. "My friend?"

I looked at his outstretched hand. I almost reached to take it. But then the memory of our dying men lying outside the walls of Acre suddenly flooded through my mind. I stared at the scimitar sheathed at his waist. How many of them had he killed?

I could not answer him. I could not move.

He flushed, a deep, dark crimson, and dropped his hand. Then he whirled away from me and disappeared into the shadows.

As I write this now I am more troubled in my mind than I have ever been in my life. Did Rashid speak the truth about Jerusalem? In all the songs and stories

I have heard about that glorious conquest of our old crusaders almost a hundred years ago, never a word was mentioned of the massacre of innocents. Did the song-makers and scribes, then, do as I did when writing of our battle? Did they leave things out? Did they make the story the way they wanted it to be? The way their lords and masters wanted it to be?

And what did Rashid mean when he said that we shared the old prophets? That we believe in the same God? How could this be?

The questions hammer at me and will not leave me in peace.

The twenty-first day of June

As I listened to the Muslim call to prayer this morning I was still mulling over Rashid's words. I had never thought of Jerusalem as being other than a Christian city, never thought about its being holy to the Muslims as well.

I'm certain our priests would condemn these thoughts as blasphemy. Are they? And do we really share the old prophets with the Muslims? I know we do with the Jews, for the Old Testament of the Bible is as much their history as ours—until the birth of Christ, of course. This much our priests have taught us. This must be what Rashid meant when he said the Christians and the Jews were people of the Book. But the Muslims too?

Then, as these new notions chased themselves around and around in my mind and the call to prayer rang on, another thought struck me. Yusra. She is Muslim. She must need to pray in the

Muslim way, but how can she in Queen Joanna's
tent? Father Aimar would never permit it. More
than that, he is probably insisting she take part in
the Christian services. I have the greatest respect for
our priests and am truly grateful for their prayers,
but I know how diligently they seek to convert those
whom they label heathen, and Father Aimar is fore-
most among them. Yusra is frail and frightened
enough. Father Aimar is so stern and forbidding, he
could not help but terrify her further. I must seek an
audience with the queen and discuss this with her.

Another thought. Do the priests know we share
the prophets with the Muslims?

The twenty-second day of June

The king continues to recover. I attended him this
morning and he was in a rage because King Philip
had made an assault on the city without consulting
him. It failed, of course.

"God's legs," he growled, "does Philip think I am
dead already that he need not advise me of his
doings?"

On the one hand I worried that he was overtaxing
himself and doing himself harm, but on the other I
figured that if he could still summon the strength to
get angry and swear, he could not be too near death.

He gave me a few small tasks to do, then
dismissed me. I determined to go straight to Queen
Joanna and speak to her about Yusra, but that was
not so easily done. It took me an hour to persuade
her lady-in-waiting to let me see her. Truly that
woman—Margaret her name is—is a dragon.

"My lady is resting," she said at first.

"She will want to see me," I replied. "She has asked me to help her with the Muslim child."

"Did she send for you?" Margaret asked, looking down her nose at me as if I were scum from the latrine ditch.

"No," I was forced to admit, "but . . ."

"If she wishes to see you," she answered, her face clearly showing how unlikely she thought this to be, "she will send for you. Besides," she added, "Her Grace has given up on that stubborn child. She is to be sent as a slave to Syria with some of the other prisoners."

My heart took a plunge. Then I had an idea.

"I have a way to make the child obey. The queen will want to know before she sends her away. I am certain of it."

We were arguing outside the doorflap of the queen's tent. I had been speaking more and more loudly, hoping that the queen would hear me. Surely, if she knew I was there she would see me. My ploy worked. A maid suddenly poked her head out of the opening.

"Is that the boy, Matthew?" she asked.

"Yes," I shot back before the dragon had a chance to open her mouth. "I would see the queen about the Muslim girl."

The maid's head disappeared for a moment, then reappeared. "Send him in," she said. "Her Grace would speak with him."

Margaret turned a most interesting shade of purple, but I darted past her into the tent.

The queen was resting on pillows at the back of the tent. There was no sign of Yusra. Nor, to my great relief, was Father Aimar there.

"Matthew," Queen Joanna said. "I am surprised to see you. What do you wish?"

"I've come about the Muslim girl, Your Grace," I replied, kneeling.

She frowned. "Truth to tell, my lad, I've given up on that child. She mopes and sulks and will not respond to any kindness shown her. Yesterday she even bit my maid when she tried to wash the girl. I fear there is no reasoning with her."

"Begging your permission, Your Grace," I said as humbly as I could, "I believe I have thought of something that might make things easier with her."

"I'm not certain I even want to try anymore, Matthew," the queen answered. "I've already decided to send her away."

"Has she left yet?" I asked. To my surprise I felt a sudden shaft of pain that took away my breath. I had not realized the girl was so important to me. Perhaps it was because I had rescued Yusra, truth to tell I do not know, but in that moment I realized I wanted desperately to save her.

"No, not yet," Queen Joanna replied.

I breathed again. "She is Muslim, Your Grace," I began, choosing my words with care.

"Yes, what of it?" the queen answered. Her frown deepened. "She would not even listen to Father Aimar when he tried to question her about her faith. He has a few words of Arabic and I'm certain she understood, but she pretended not to. I fear she is too obdurate to be reasoned with."

"She must pray. Five times a day. It is necessary for her."

"She could pray with Father Aimar whenever she wanted," the queen replied.

I took a deep breath. I was very frightened of what I was about to say next. It would have been much more prudent of me not to say it, but I am not always prudent.

"She must pray in her own way." The words came out in a rush. "It is to the same God, but she is Muslim. She must pray in the Muslim way."

"The same God!" The queen glanced quickly around. "What blasphemy are you speaking, Matthew? Be glad Father Aimar is not here to hear you!"

"But it's true, Your Grace. I have spoken with a Muslim boy. He told me. They share the old prophets with us. They believe that the archangel Gabriel is the messenger of God, as we do . . ." I stopped. The queen looked horrified. It would undoubtedly have been better if I had had the sense to stay stopped but, as I have already noted, I do not always do the prudent or sensible thing.

"If you could let her pray, Your Grace, in her own way, at her own times, perhaps she would be more content with us. The Muslims in Sicily, Your Grace, they prayed side by side with the Christians. It did no harm . . ."

"Did no harm? Matthew! I can only surmise that you are so young and have received so little education that you do not know what you are saying. The Muslims are infidels, and the Kingdom of Heaven is denied to them. Are we to encourage this young child in her heresy? We should, rather, be doing all in our power to help her learn the true way, that her soul may be saved."

I stood mute before her. Of course all that she said was true. What answer could I possibly make?

So why now do I feel so miserable? Why can I not sleep? Why do I feel so guilty?

The twenty-third day of June

I could not help myself. I went again to the queen's pavilion this morning. The dragon, thanks be to God, was not there. The queen did not smile when she received me this time. I knelt before her and could not look anywhere else but at the ground.

"Please, Your Grace," I said. "Please do not send Yusra into slavery in Syria." My voice wobbled and came out so weakly that at first I was afraid she had not heard me. Then on a last, desperate impulse I forced myself to look up straight into her eyes.

"If we keep her with us, if we keep trying, perhaps we can teach her the true faith. Perhaps we can save her," I pleaded.

The queen looked back at me and I felt as if she were reading the thoughts in my brain as easily as she would the words on a parchment scroll.

"I would like to believe you mean that, Matthew," she said quietly.

"I do, Your Grace. I do!" I said fervently.

But do I? Or was I just saying what I had to in

order to save Yusra? I do not even know myself. But the words worked. Yusra will not be sent away. And I am to speak to her tomorrow and explain things to her. The most I can hope for is that I can persuade her not to bite.

Why *am* I so concerned with this child?

The twenty-fourth day of June

A difficult interview. That girl is indeed stubborn. But so am I. Luckily the queen allowed me to speak to her alone.

"If you continue to be so obstinate you will be sent away as a slave," I said to her.

"Then a slave I will be," she retorted. She no longer cries but is as angry as a wasp.

"It will go much worse for you as a slave than as a maidservant to Queen Joanna," I insisted.

"That priest, he wants me to embrace your Christian religion. I cannot do that."

"You would not even be given the choice as a slave," I answered. I was beginning to get annoyed in spite of myself. "You would be worked to death. You would be raped. Your life would be a misery. You would probably be dead within the year." The words were harsh, I knew, but I had to make her understand.

She flinched, then glared at me. "I would rather be dead. If it is God's will that this is what I must endure, then I will endure it."

"There might be a way," I said. The words pushed themselves out even as I was telling myself not to say them. "If you behave," I said slowly, "if you at least pretend to go along with the queen's wishes, perhaps I could do something sometime . . ."

She leaped on my words like a dog on a bone. "You could get me back to my own people?" Her face suddenly came alive.

"I can't promise you that." The light went out of her eyes. I could not bear it. "But you would have a chance . . ." I was almost begging. Again I wondered, why was I doing this? The girl meant nothing to me. Then I pushed the thought aside. Lately I do not understand anything, least of all myself.

"Promise me then that you will at least try to help me," she said. "If I could have some hope . . . Promise me that and I will promise you to do my best here."

I squirmed. This was not what I had had in mind. I only wanted her to do what was necessary to make life easier for herself. Yusra, however, does not seem too concerned with that. With her staring at me in such a manner, with such hope in her eyes, what could I do? I gave up.

"I will try," I said.

"Promise?" She was relentless.

I gave up completely. "I promise," I said.

She smiled. "And I promise I won't bite the maid again. As long as she doesn't try to wash me. I will wash myself. Besides, these Christians are filthy. They do not wash before praying, they do not even wash after relieving themselves. I would not let one of them touch me. Tell them that."

God's legs, I thought, what have I got myself into

now? But I was right. She is very pretty when she smiles.

The twenty-fifth day of June

I was summoned to the queen's pavilion early this morning, before the breaking of the fast.

"You will attend morning mass with Father Aimar here in my tent from now on," she informed me sternly. I think, after our conversation the other day, she is worried about my soul.

Besides Father Aimar, all the queen's ladies and maidservants were there. Queen Berengaria attended as well, not looking any happier than she had the last time I saw her. The gossip in the camp is that the king rarely bothers himself with her. I suppose matters of war take precedence, but it must be hard for her.

Yusra was sitting beside the queen. She knelt with the rest of us as Father Aimar began the prayers, but I saw that while we faced the priest, she knelt sideways to him. Facing south, toward Mecca. No one else noticed, but it seems Yusra has found a way to pray her own way.

When Father Aimar finished saying the mass I started to leave. I knew the king would be expecting me. He is getting better day by day and I have begun my regular work again. The priest stopped me, however.

"Wait, Matthew," he said. "I would speak with you."

The queen and her ladies left, taking Yusra with them. The girl cast a glance at me, obviously curious as to what business I had with the priest and probably wondering if it had aught to do with her. In a way, it did.

"Her Grace has informed me that you have been talking with a Muslim boy," Father Aimar began.

I cleared my throat before answering. I must admit, I was more than a little frightened of him. I had never spoken to him before.

"I have, Father," I answered. I wondered what was coming next. Surely it was no sin to converse with a Muslim. It had been happening in the camp for the last two years. What had the queen told him? I tried desperately to remember exactly what I had said. I have heard tales of those who have been punished for blaspheming—unpleasant tales. My mouth was suddenly dry.

"Her Grace says you are confused about their religion," he went on.

"I . . . I was surprised to learn they revere the same prophets we do, Father," I managed to get out. "And the archangel Gabriel."

He stared down at me. I had thought the queen's gaze was piercing, but it was nothing compared to his. I knew beyond a doubt that I would never be able to keep any thought from this holy man. To lie to him would be inconceivable.

"They do," he said.

I was surprised. I had expected him to deny it.

"The people of Islam are a cultured people, Matthew," he said. "They study and write most wonderfully. They have a rich history. But they are a people who have lost their way. They deny that our Lord Jesus Christ is the Son of God. They hold him to be nothing more than one of the prophets." To my intense discomfort he reached out and put a hand on my shoulder.

"They are misguided, Matthew. They are blasphemous heathens. Do not forget that." He gave me a little push. "Now, go to the king. Do your duties and while you do, give thanks to God, the only true God, that you walk in the path of truth and will be saved."

I wrote lists and letters for King Richard and tallied supplies and worked all day, but my mind did not cease whirling around like a spinning top.

The Jews worship one God. The Muslims worship one God. We worship one God. Could it not be, as Rashid said, the same God? And if it is, then which of us have blasphemed and lost our way and which of us have found the truth? Or could it be that none of us have blasphemed? Could it be that we have each found the truth in our own way?

I have lost some of my fear of Father Aimar. Indeed, I think I will enjoy hearing mass from him each morning. But somehow I do not think I will dare to ask him these questions.

The twenty-sixth day of June

King Richard had himself carried in a litter around the battle lines today. He is still weak and pale almost to death, but he did not let that stop him from cheering the men on and exhorting them to greater and greater efforts. I limped along behind him and I could see how his words filled the men with courage. They cheered him back with loud huzzahs. When we approached the soldiers they looked bowed and dispirited, but as the king passed I could see backs straighten and faces lighten. Truly, this king's men love him dearly. As do I.

The twenty-seventh day of June

The work of undermining the walls of Acre is going on at a great pace now that the king is well again. Our siege engines and mangonels keep up a steady barrage by day, and by night men dig under the walls and set fires within them. The Saracens repair the damage as much as they can, but I can see that they are falling behind. Slowly the walls are coming down, and every time a section of wall collapses our forces follow up with an attack. The defenders then beat drums as a signal and Salah-ud-Din's army streams down upon us from behind. We are still forced to fight on two fronts, but the defenders are becoming weaker and weaker.

A tower was undermined so severely last night that this morning it seems on the verge of toppling. The king is so eager to see it fall that he has offered two bezants to anyone who can bring him back a stone. To do this a man must cross the moat, so the ditch is fast being filled in with rubble and all kinds of rubbish. Some of the people have become so crazed that they stand brazenly along the edge of the moat and throw stones at the walls, ignoring the arrows that rain down upon them. I even saw a woman with a bow standing full out in the open and shooting at the soldiers on the parapets above her.

Miraculously she held out for almost half of an hour before she was brought down. Her body lies where it fell. Perhaps the king should offer two bezants to the man who can retrieve it.

Yesterday more French ships arrived and have now blockaded the harbor. This means that the Muslim ships can no longer deliver supplies to the city of Acre, and the townspeople's stores must be running low. It seems that victory might actually be in sight.

The first day of July

The fighting has been stepped up. Every day now we attack the city. Salah-ud-Din's forces continue to harass us from behind, but the city offers less and less resistance. We are losing many men though.

The second day of July

We go from horror to horror. The air is filled from dawn to dusk with the cries of the dying and the agony of the wounded who lie stranded on the ground between us and the city walls after each foray. We live with the stench of blood, sweat and death in the heat of the summer sun. The flies are so thick they are enough to drive a man crazy.

The fourth day of July

Salah-ud-Din attacked with the dawn. This time he had no help from the city at all and our army repelled him with ease. The walls are crumbling everywhere and the moat has been almost filled in. This siege cannot go on much longer.

The twelfth day of July

The city has surrendered! The white flag was hoisted over the walls this morning and King Richard and King Philip have ridden triumphantly in. Of Salah-ud-Din there is no sign.

The siege of Acre is over!

The thirteenth day of July

I am suddenly overwhelmed with work. The king summoned me late last night and set me to copying out the terms of the surrender. The lives of the defenders and the soldiers we have captured are to be spared in return for a ransom of two hundred thousand gold dinars and the release of the thousand or so prisoners that Salah-ud-Din holds. The Muslim sultan is also in possession of the True Cross, which he stole from Jerusalem, and this must be returned. Messengers have ridden from the city to inform Salah-ud-Din of this agreement, but he has sent no answer as yet. Here in the camp, we await the sultan's reaction with a certain amount of nervousness, but with our forces in possession of the city he must give in.

So it is over—the first part of our crusade at least. There is still a long way to go before we reach Jerusalem, however.

I cannot help but admire the spirit of these men behind the walls of Acre. For two years they lived under siege and would not give up. I am not alone in my admiration either. I wrote a letter for King Richard today, addressed to the Pope himself, informing His Eminence of our great victory. In it the king said, "What can we say of this race of infidels who thus defended their city? Never were there braver soldiers than these, the honor of their nation. If only they had been of the true faith it would not have been possible to find anywhere in the world men to surpass them."

I wonder where Rashid is. What part did he play in all this?

The fourteenth day of July

The reports are that Salah-ud-Din is furious over the surrender of Acre and most especially over the terms. There is nothing he can do, however. He must acquiesce.

We moved into the city today. King Richard and Queen Berengaria have taken up residence in a tall three-storied house near the main gate. I think it must have belonged to the commander of the garrison. Maybe now the king will pay more attention to his wife. I have been given a whole room to myself! Queen Joanna occupies a smaller house beside it and Yusra dwells there with her. I have not been able to see her since we moved, but I will try as soon as we have settled into these new quarters.

The first order of the day is the reconsecration of the Christian churches. Our priests have started in on that with a vengeance. The king is firing off letters non-stop and my hand aches from the writing of them.

Apparently King Philip is demanding more than his share of the booty of this conquest. He and King Richard are arguing again. Nothing new in that.

As soon as I have the opportunity, I am going to sneak away and investigate this city for myself. What I have seen of it so far intrigues me. Never before have I dwelt in such a small, walled-in town. The streets are narrow and twisting. Already I have lost myself twice, just running errands for the king. The soldiers that garrisoned the city have all been taken prisoner. Those who will convert to Christianity will be given their freedom as long as they promise to stay and fight for us. The others will be imprisoned. I have heard there are vast chambers and dungeons underneath the city where they will be held. Those I must see! The ordinary citizens have been given permission to leave or stay, as they wish. Most have left, so our people are busily occupying their houses, but a good number remain. Already the marketplace has been reestablished and we are being supplied by the French ships in the harbor, which is just as well. The people here must have been close to starving, for there is precious little food available.

King Richard has given strict orders that the Muslim population here is not to be persecuted. He has learned from the lessons of the past, I think. He is even allowing them to pray as usual, but not in the churches that they seized from the Christians when they took Acre, of course. Those are the churches that are being reconsecrated to Christ.

The fifteenth day of July

The soldiers who converted to Christianity bolted for the Muslim army in the hills as soon as they were set free. Their conversion was only a pretense, and no more prisoners will be given that option. The nobles here heap scorn upon them for deceiving us, but really it is no more than what our own King Guy of Jerusalem did. According to my good source, Rigord, when Salah-ud-Din defeated King Guy at the Battle of the Horns of Hattim, when Jerusalem was lost to the Saracens, Salah-ud-Din spared the king's life and set him free upon his promise that he would not take up arms against the sultan again. No sooner did King Guy reach the safety of his own lines, however, than the priests declared that an oath given to an infidel was worthless and delivered him from it. He has been fighting with us ever since. What is treachery to one side is honorable behavior to the other, it seems.

I have been dismissed from duty with the king for the day. I am now going to explore!

Later . . .

I have made a terrible discovery. But I will hold back and force myself to write everything down as it happened.

I stowed my writing materials away with glee and set out to explore, not even stopping for a morsel to eat although I had had nothing since yesterday evening. At first I was enthralled by the strangeness of it all. I am used to walls around a city, but not so close. The city of Acre is, in truth, a fortress, built on a promontory of land. On three sides there is water. The harbor is on the eastern side. It is wide and deep and protected from the storms and currents that come up from the south by a breakwater made of huge blocks of stones. It must be one of the finest and safest harbors in the world. A wondrous prize for our armies, indeed.

The city itself is a maze of streets, paved mostly with cobblestones. As I wandered among the market stalls the smells of cooking awoke my appetite, and I spent some of my coins on fruit and fresh, hot bread. There were also stalls selling pottery and weaving, copper and silver ornaments. Most of these stall owners are Muslim and seem to be prepared to live with us in peace as long as we leave them alone. They are selling off all manner of other goods as well, such as old clothing and bits of furniture, desperate to get money to buy the food and supplies that are now pouring into the city. These people have a hungry look to them. Truly, life in this city during the siege must have been hard. But now there is noise and bustle and liveliness. It seems a wonder that the memory of war can be obliterated so quickly. It was not so in Jerusalem, I warrant, after our crusaders took that city.

Many of the streets have arches running across them with yet more buildings built on their tops. There are layers and layers to the city, and the walls are old. I saw whole trees growing out of the cracks between the stones. The trunks jut out sideways, against the laws of nature, and then the branches turn and reach for the sky. Most odd. Flowering bushes cascade down the walls in many places, creating curtains of beauty. Palm trees and orange trees grow in green nooks and crannies. Altogether this would be a lovely place if it were not for the filth underfoot everywhere and the smell.

I am still reeling with the shock of my discovery, but writing this description down is helping to calm me. I will continue.

Soon the sun was beating down on the city unmercifully and I began to look for a shady spot in which to enjoy my fruit and bread. I saw a nook in the corner of an empty courtyard formed by the meeting of the outside wall with one of the street walls. Vines filled the corner and I thought it might offer a cool shelter. I made my way toward it and then saw that the vines were covering a small open-ing. A dank, damp smell assailed my wounded nose. It was pitch dark inside. I could just barely make out a few steps leading down into the black-ness. Most mysterious. My curiosity was immedi-ately aroused. I stuffed the bread into my mouth, tucked the fruit into my tunic and pushed my way through.

Once I was on the other side of the vines and looking down the stairs I could see a glimmer of light at the other end. That was all I needed to encourage me. I felt for the wall to steady me, and started down. The steps were rough and uneven. I had to go slowly to ensure that I did not trip. Finally I came to a level place and there the stairway divided, with one branch leading off to the right, another to the left. The glimmer of light I had seen came from the right-hand one, so I chose that. It was a short tunnel that burrowed through the stone of the wall, then ended in an opening. The whole passageway smelled clammy and deserted. It occurred to me that probably no one had been this way for years. At the end an iron grate had loosened from its fastening and hung askew. I looked out the opening and then drew back as my stomach took a lurch. I was far above the harbor waters. The waves dashed in below me and hurled themselves toward the shore.

I retraced my steps and decided to try the other branch. Stairs led down toward the inside of the fort. I descended slowly and carefully, taking care that my treacherous foot did not cause me to trip. It was so dark I could not see at all, so I felt cautiously for each step before advancing. As I descended lower and lower I began to hear voices and what sounded like moans and muffled cries. The stairs took a bend, then ended in another grating. This one was firmly in place. I crept as close as I could to it and peered through.

I was looking down into a vast cavern of a room, dim and flickering with torchlight. Pillars supported arches that curved far above. Opposite me I could make out a doorway and beyond that yet another dark, cavernous room. Both rooms were filled with men and it was they who were murmuring and crying out. Some were lying on pallets, others were striding restlessly about.

They were soldiers. Muslim soldiers. I had found the dungeons where the prisoners were being held.

I knelt, allowing my eyes to get used to the dim light. I was searching for one familiar figure—a figure I did not want to find. After a long while, once I had scrutinized each and every man as closely as I could, I let out a sigh of relief. As far as I could see Rashid was not here. Of course, there were other rooms and many more prisoners I could not see, but at least I had not found him. Yet.

I cast one last glance around, then looked down. A man was leaning against the wall just below me. All I could see of him was the top of his crimson turban. As I watched, he walked a few steps out into the room, then turned and faced the grill. It was Rashid!

Later still . . .

I had to stop. My hand was cramping and my wick burning low. It is so late now that the whole city lies silent and sleeping. I cannot sleep, however.

Rashid must have seen the pale outline of my face behind the bars at the same moment as I saw him. His mouth fell open with surprise. Quickly I raised a finger to my lips and signaled him to remain quiet. Thanks be to God, he did. He collected himself, then glanced quickly around. There was no one else near and no one was paying any attention to him. Only then did he allow himself to approach the grate.

"Rashid," I hissed. "It is I, Matthew."

He had enough wits about him to amble slowly up to the wall, then turn and lean against it again.

"How came you here?" he muttered, so low I could barely hear him.

"I found a passage," I answered.

"Does it lead to the outside?" he asked quickly.

"It does," I answered.

"Could I escape through it then?"

I bit my lip. "The grating is solid here. I do not know if I could loosen it." Even as I spoke the words my mind was racing. Rashid was a prisoner. An enemy. It would be traitorous of me to help him escape. I could not do that. And yet . . . And yet he had undoubtedly saved my life. Did I not owe him the same in return?

But my help was not what he wanted.

"I did not ask for your assistance," he snapped, his tone as cold as ice.

I flushed. I knew he was remembering my refusal to take his hand in friendship at our last meeting.

"The grate is set too firmly in place," I whispered. "Even if you could manage to loosen it, there is no way out for you. I am in a tunnel with two branches. One leads to a hole high above the sea, too far for you to jump even if you can swim. The other branch comes up inside the city. If you tried to escape that way you would be caught immediately."

Rashid shrugged. "Then there is no use talking further," he said. "You had better go."

"I'm sorry," I began, but what could I say?

"It is of no consequence," he answered. "Go."

A man nearby looked over at Rashid curiously. Had he heard him speak? This was getting too dangerous.

"I will," I said quickly, "but I'll be back. Tomorrow. At this same time. Wait for me here."

Without waiting for his reply I melted back into

the shadows and stumbled up the stairs. The heat of the sun felt blessedly welcome as I finally emerged into the dazzle of the courtyard.

What am I to do? I cannot leave him there. But to help him, even if I could, would be treason. Besides, he obviously does not trust me now and does not want my help.

What am I to do?

The sixteenth day of July

I woke up this morning with a plan. With two plans, truth to tell, although I was not too certain about the second one. I was determined to help Rashid escape, and I believed I knew how to persuade him to accept my help. I owe him my life, so I must do this. But I resolved that he had to give me his word that he would not involve any of the other prisoners. I can justify saving his life because he saved mine, but I cannot justify setting free any of the other Muslim soldiers.

Late this afternoon I made my way back to the hidden cranny in the courtyard. This time I took with me the dagger I use for cutting meat when I eat. I crept down the dark stairs and peered into the dungeon. I did not see Rashid, but set to work anyway. I began working around the grate with the point of my dagger, loosening it wherever possible. I worked as quietly as I could so as not to attract the attention of any of the prisoners. I was so immersed in my work that a sudden whisper startled me. Rashid was leaning against the wall below.

"What are you doing?" he asked, his voice muffled.

"I'm loosening the grate," I whispered.

"I said I did not want your assistance," he hissed. "Besides, you said there was no way out for me."

I had thought long and hard last night about what I should say to him.

"I want to help you," I replied. "You saved my life and I repaid that debt with an insult. I did not mean to and would not do so again, but I was in shock over the aftermath of the battle. That is no excuse, I know, but now I must help you and I have worked out a plan. Please let me tell it to you and then you may decide."

"What is it?" The tone of his voice was still cold, but I was sure I could detect a hint of interest in it. I took heart.

"If I can get this grate off," I said, "you must go through it when no one is watching you and then take the branch of the tunnel that leads up into the city. Dressed as you are now, in the garb of a Muslim soldier, you would have no chance, but if you were clothed as a simple farmer you could mingle with the crowds in the market and then make your way out the gate. The guards check all who come in closely, but they do not bother much with those going out."

"Where would I get such clothing?" Rashid asked. There was definitely a growing interest in his voice. I hurried on.

"I will buy it for you in the market," I said. I had counted the few coins I had hoarded away in my pack, made some inquiries and knew I had enough to buy him an old, used robe. "I could bring a robe down here, bundle it up and leave it in the passageway. When you got out you could change, and creep up the stairs and into the courtyard. If you escaped at night you could hide in the courtyard until morning, then slip out and mingle with the Muslim people in the market. Those who wish to leave the city are still being allowed out with no checks, so you could make your way to the gate and leave. I do not think there would be a problem."

"What about the others?" He cast a quick glance around. "I could not leave my fellow soldiers."

This was what I had feared.

"No." I shook my head although he could not see me. "If more than one of you try to escape you will all be caught. Besides, I can procure no more than one robe."

"If all of us escape, there are enough of us to fight our way out." His voice was suddenly hard.

I stopped my work. "If all of you escape and you fight your way out, many Christians will be killed. I can justify helping you escape, but I cannot justify that." I made my voice just as hard. "If I do not have your word that you will do this alone, I will work no further. I will not help you escape."

"And you believe I would honor my word?" he asked quietly.

"I know you would," I said.

And I do believe that. If I am wrong, then God have mercy on me for I will have the deaths of many innocent people on my soul. But I do believe that Rashid will honor his word.

"I cannot leave them," Rashid said then. "*That* would not be honorable."

"They will be traded for the Christian prisoners that the sultan holds," I said. "That was part of the treaty."

"Then I should wait with them," he answered.

"Would it not be wiser for you to escape if you can?" I was desperate to convince him. "You could carry word back to your sultan about the condition of your soldiers here. Persuade him to go ahead with the exchange of prisoners as soon as possible. You would do them more of a favor that way, I am certain of it." I had another reason for wanting Rashid to escape and that had to do with my second plan, which I then broached. "Moreover," I said, "if you escape now, you could help a Muslim child escape as well."

Rashid stiffened. I could see he was restraining himself with difficulty from turning and looking up at me. "What do you mean?" he asked.

I told him about Yusra. "She is not happy here and will never be happy here. I am afraid that eventually the queen will lose patience with her and send her off into slavery," I said. "Besides, if you have a child with you, the guards will take even less notice of you."

Rashid was silent for a several long moments. I dug away at the grating and bit my lip in order to keep silent while he made his decision. Finally he spoke.

"Yes," he said. "I could take her with me. I could give her into the care of my aunt. She would be well taken care of and she should be with our people. It must be torture for her to live amongst you Christians. And our sultan must be told how desperate we are here." He took a few restless paces away from the grating, then whirled and paced back. He leaned against the wall again. "I will do it then. But how?"

One whole side of the grating came free.

"I will get this grate free by tomorrow, I'm certain," I replied. "Tomorrow night I will come back with Yusra." I stopped for a moment. I had not yet worked out how I would accomplish that, but I plowed on in any case. I would solve that problem when I came to it. Then an even greater problem presented itself. "Will you be able to climb up through the grate unobserved?" I asked.

"At night they take away the torches. It is deepest black in here then," Rashid answered. "No one would see."

I let out a sigh of relief. "Good," I said. "I will work away here today as long as I can, then return tomorrow and finish. Tomorrow night you will be free."

By the time I left the grate was almost completely loose. It will be no problem at all to do the rest of the work tomorrow.

Now I am pondering how I will get Yusra away from the queen's house. It should not be too difficult. I know the girl sleeps in the back, in the cooking area. The door is bolted at night, but she would be able to open it from the inside. I will make occasion to speak with her tomorrow and tell her to wait for me as soon as night falls and be ready to flee with me. She is so anxious to return to her own people I am certain she will comply. We will have to avoid the guards, but I know where they are stationed so that will not be difficult.

It occurs to me that helping Yusra is probably just as traitorous as helping Rashid, but I intend to do it anyway.

The seventeenth day of July

That silly, impatient girl! She has ruined everything. For herself at least.

I awoke this morning and reported to the king as usual, but his household was in a tizzy. It seems that Yusra tried to creep out of the queen's house early this morning and was caught by one of the guards. The queen was furious. After I finished my duties with the king I asked leave to go to Queen Joanna's house and see the girl. It was granted, but reluctantly.

"That ungrateful little wretch," the queen snapped as I made my bow to her. "After all we have done for her she tries to sneak away at the first opportunity."

"May I speak with her, Your Grace?" I asked as humbly as I could.

The queen turned to one of her maidservants. "Bring the child in," she ordered.

Yusra entered, pushed ahead by the maid. She had obviously been crying. Her eyes were red and swollen.

"What happened, Yusra?" I asked. "What did you think you were doing?"

"I did not think," she answered. "I heard the

adhan, the call to morning prayer, and I knew my people were just outside this house and I had to go to them. I had to!"

"But you know no one here. How would you know where to go? How could you be certain the Muslims here would accept you? Take care of you?" I said.

She looked at me as if I were the child. "It matters not if other Muslims know me, Matthew. They would take me in and care for me, just because I am Muslim. All I would have to do would be to say, 'Ashadu an lailaha illallahu, Muhammadur rasullal-lah'—I bear witness that there is no god but God and Muhammad is his messenger—and they would recognize me and care for me immediately. Would not your Christians do the same?"

I could not answer. Truth, I was not certain they would. Certainly no one had shown me any kindness when I was left alone after the death of my parents. Vulgrin had only taken me on as apprentice because of his promise to my father—that and the fact that he could get a great deal of work out of me for very little compensation. Before I could collect my thoughts, Queen Joanna broke in.

"We have been too lenient with her, Matthew. She will be bolted into a room with my most trusted servants at night from now on. This must not happen again."

It crossed my mind that the queen had been willing to let this girl be sent into slavery. Why would she not now just let Yusra go? It was not a thought I could express though. I have come to know Queen

Joanna well enough to understand that although she is the most kindly of ladies, she has inherited the same pride and stubbornness as her brother, the king. Both of them are always certain that they know best and cannot be turned once they have set their mind to a matter. Queen Joanna seems determined to save this child, according to her beliefs. I am sure she would deem it a sin to return the child to the infidels now.

Is it? By helping her to escape, would I be sinful as well as traitorous? My life is becoming very confusing.

It was with a heavy heart that I returned to Rashid's prison late this afternoon. I took with me a robe that I purchased at one of the market stalls. It was old and smelly and very ragged. Rashid would not be comfortable in it, I was certain. And I was afraid that once he knew he would not be able to save Yusra, he would refuse to go.

My fears were justified. He was waiting for me when I arrived. His face was grim and he was staring at his fellow warriors with a frown.

"I have the robe," I whispered. "It is here beside the grate." Then, as quickly as I could, I told him what had happened to Yusra. As I spoke I continued to work and the grate suddenly came free. It almost fell to the ground, but I caught it just in time and propped it back in place.

Rashid did not seem to notice. He was still staring at his comrades. "That is unfortunate," he said without turning around. "The child should be with us. She will never be happy with you."

"I know," I answered.

"This changes the situation," he said then. "Perhaps I should stay after all. I should not leave my fellow men here."

"But King Richard and King Philip are getting impatient," I whispered urgently. "You must tell your sultan that."

He hesitated still.

"If I could only be certain that I am doing the right thing," he muttered.

"You are," I insisted. "I am sure of it." I was desperate for him to agree.

He sighed, then straightened his shoulders as if he had come to a decision. "Very well. I will go. But there is no need now for you to return tonight," he went on. "When all is quiet and the torches have been taken away I will make my own way out."

I was about to object, then stopped. He was right, but every bit of me protested. I wanted to be there to help him.

He looked directly up at me then. "I spoke harshly to you, Matthew," he said. "I should not have done so."

"You had good reason," I said.

We stared at each other silently, knowing full well that this was most likely the last time our paths would cross.

"Assalamu alaikum," he said finally.

This time I answered with all my heart. "And peace be with you," I replied.

I left and did not go back. It is late now and dark. I wonder if he has made his escape.

The eighteenth day of July

There was no outcry over any escaped prisoner. If Rashid did make it out, no one has noticed.

Later . . .

I returned to the staircase this evening. The robe is gone, the grate stuck firmly back in place. There has been no news of any escaped prisoner being captured. I can only believe that Rashid is free and safe.

I suppose I should feel guilty about what I have done, but I do not. It was necessary.

The twentieth day of July

I have been working from early morning to late at night with the king. There has been no time to see Yusra. I know not how she fares, but I fear that she is very unhappy.

King Philip is meeting daily with King Richard and the two kings squabble incessantly over the spoils we have captured in this city. Now yet another matter has arisen to divide them even further. Both King Guy of Jerusalem and Conrad of Montferrat, who contests Guy for the kingship, have formally submitted claims as king of Jerusalem. I deem the matter ridiculous as even though we have captured Acre, we are still a very long way from recapturing Jerusalem, but no one has asked for my opinion. Of course, King Philip supports Conrad and King Richard maintains that Guy is still the rightful king, even though he lost the city to the Saracens. King Richard's rooms are filled with angry voices and shouted insults and I am supposed to record it all faithfully. No, not faithfully. When I wrote down the arguments as I heard them, insults and all, King Richard ordered me to leave out the vituperation. History is not to know what a wealth of swear words both kings possess, I see.

Meanwhile King Richard is busy having his coat of arms chiseled into the walls throughout the city and King Philip is just as industriously inscribing his. King Richard's lions and King Philip's fleurs-de-lis sit defiantly next to each other in some places and menace each other from opposing sides of archways in others. I have begun to see another emblem as well, one that is not so controversial. It shows two arms, crossed, with the palms of the hands open and facing forward. Between the hands sits a cross with four smaller crosses filling the spaces between its branches. People are calling it the Crusader Cross. It is a pleasing emblem, I think.

The twenty-ninth day of July

King Philip is ill. He is talking about leaving!

The thirty-first day of July

King Philip has left Acre. Conrad has gone with him to Tyre, then King Philip will set sail for France. His departure is being looked upon by most of the crusaders as a treacherous desertion and a cowardly failure to fulfill his pilgrim's vow. I hear talk that he has been even more traitorous and has been secretly negotiating a treaty with Salah-ud-Din. King

Richard does not believe this to be true, however, as King Philip took only three galleys with him and left the rest of his army and treasure here for Duke Hugh of Burgundy.

King Richard, in fact, does not seem as angry as he might have been. He is now the supreme commander of all the crusading forces and, in his own words, King Philip was to him "like a hammer tied to the tail of a cat." A weapon that was often out of control.

All efforts are now being made to see that Salah-ud-Din implements the terms of the treaty made by his officers at Acre. I wonder if Rashid is there. If he is, I know he will be working to ensure that his fellow soldiers are released as soon as possible. Why is Salah-ud-Din taking so long? Perhaps he is having trouble collecting such a large sum of money and bringing together all of the prisoners captured by the Muslim forces. The first install-ment of the ransom must be paid by the twentieth day of August, however. King Richard is inflexible about that.

The nineteenth day of August

We have had nothing to do but wait these past weeks. I have not even written in this journal as I keep expecting something to happen, but there has been no move by Salah-ud-Din to pay the ransom or release the prisoners. Indeed, a rumor is running wildly through our camp that he has killed them all. I do not believe it. The mood here is ugly, however. King Richard is champing at the bit to leave Acre and march on to Jerusalem, but he cannot leave three thousand Muslim soldiers here as prisoners. There would simply not be enough men to guard them. Also, Salah-ud-Din holds the True Cross from Jerusalem in his possession and he steadfastly refuses to even discuss returning it. The cross is too good a bargaining tool, it seems.

King Richard has been conferring with the other nobles late into the night. I was dismissed shortly after they arrived. That is unusual. What is transpiring that the king wants no record of?

The twentieth day of August

I do not know how to write this. Indeed, King Richard has not asked me to and I wonder if he will. But I have to record what has happened, even though to do so causes me anguish. I will set down an account here in my own journal.

It seems that the king's council last night came to a terrible decision. By noon today, the deadline, Salah-ud-Din's envoys had not appeared with either ransom or prisoners, much less with the True Cross. At that hour trumpets sounded and King Richard marched his army out of Acre. They formed what looked to be a guard of honor on the fields outside the walls. I ran to a spot I know of on top of one of the walls where I could see what was going on. I had no idea what would happen next.

What did happen was that all three thousand prisoners were marched out and arranged in rows before the soldiers. The wounded were dragged out on litters. They stayed there, in the searing

midday heat, for several long moments. No one
moved. I could not believe the silence that
descended on the field. Then the trumpets
sounded again and with ear-splitting war cries the
soldiers fell upon the prisoners. They hacked and
slashed. The prisoners screamed. I watched,
unable to turn my head away, until not one
Muslim soldier was left alive.

The priests, at mass this evening, explained it to
us. "The lives of unbelievers are of no account," they
said. "They are, in any case, doomed to hell." It
seemed that they even believed there to be virtue in
our hastening the process. "The Christian glories in
the death of a pagan," Father Aimar preached,
"because thereby Christ himself is glorified."

I think about the gentle teaching of our Lord
Jesus, the Christ, and I cannot believe this. I must
weep.

How will Rashid feel when he hears about this?
He will think he deserted his fellow soldiers and left
them to their deaths. For the rest of his life he will
carry with him the guilt of having escaped this
execution. And he will blame me. He will never
forgive me for helping him escape. When he thinks
of me now, it will be with hatred because of what I
persuaded him to do.

The twenty-first day of August

We march tomorrow for Jerusalem. King Richard
will wait no longer for Salah-ud-Din to honor the
truce agreement. Indeed, after the massacre of the
Muslim soldiers, there is no possibility of his doing

so. This means, of course, that the Christian prisoners held by the sultan will probably be massacred as well.

I was summoned to the king's pavilion early this morning. He was unshaven—very unusual for him—and very curt with me.

"Write this," he commanded. "On the twentieth day of August, after we had waited in vain for the Muslim Salah-ud-Din to exchange prisoners according to the terms of the truce agreement, the Muslim prisoners were executed."

"That is all?" I stammered.

He glared at me. "That is all. What more is there?" Then he dismissed me.

What more is there? The bodies of the Muslim soldiers lie rotting in the sun outside our gates. No doubt the bodies of our soldiers lie dead in the hills above us. All these men, some no older than I, slaughtered. Those details may not be important enough to be recorded in King Richard's history, but they will be in mine.

The twenty-second day of August

King Richard led the crusading army out of Acre this morning. It was an impressive sight. Trumpets sounded, banners flew. The procession was colorful, gaudy and noisy. Triumphant. We picked our way around the bodies.

I was called to the king's pavilion at the break of day. There, a surprise awaited me.

"I must have you by my side," the king said. "Can you ride?"

"Oh, yes," I answered. Actually, I can't, but I figured riding couldn't be too hard. Get up on the back of a horse and just sit there. I know now that there is a deal more to it than that. Fortunately I did not fall off, but I had to hang on for my life whenever the beast broke into the least kind of a trot, and I will sleep on my stomach tonight. I have blisters the size of copper coins on my backside. How I will ride again tomorrow I do not know, but I will. To ride at the side of the king of England— never in my wildest imaginings could I ever have thought of that.

My mind is in a welter of confusion though. I still admire King Richard. He is the world's greatest soldier, I believe that. But how could he murder those men? Death in battle I can begin to understand, but a cold-blooded execution such as that?

We must get on with the crusade. I know we could not have left those prisoners behind in Acre. My mind can provide all the rational arguments, but it also shows me pictures of death.

King Richard, it would seem, thinks no more about it. Only about the path we must take now.

The twenty-third day of August

I am in such pain that I cannot think. I had to take the king's dictation this evening standing up. He raised his eyebrows at that, but said nothing. He did, however, direct me to speak to his doctor when we were finished. The healer gave me a salve which is helping, I hope.

The twenty-fourth day of August

The pain has subsided somewhat. The blisters are healing.

The twenty-sixth day of August

My backside is toughening up. I am also finding it easier to ride my horse and roll with the motion. Now that my brain is not totally centered on the pain in my rear I find that riding is most enjoyable. I am even sitting as I write this—on a pillow, mind, but sitting.

King Richard has chosen to lead us down the coast to Jaffa. From there we will head inland to Jerusalem. It would have been foolhardy to head directly for the Holy City, he explained. The land is hilly and we depend on the ships that follow along beside us for our supplies. We are no longer safe behind fortifications or walls, however, and it is certain that the Turkish cavalry is keeping pace with us in the hills on the landward side. I am hearing tales from the old campaigners about the renown of this Turkish cavalry. Everyone who has come up against it speaks of it with awe. The Turks never had a real opportunity to demonstrate their cavalry skills at Acre, but here, in open country, we are at their mercy. How long will they allow us to proceed before they attack? I cannot help thinking that this time, if there is a battle, I will not be watching from a hilltop or a parapet. I will be in it.

The king has not allowed any women other than washerwomen to accompany us. The two queens

and, of course, Yusra have stayed in Acre. I hope
Yusra will do nothing foolish.

I wonder now about this Holy War we have
embarked on. "God wills it!" is the battle cry we
ride with. We must believe that. If we do not, it is
all insanity.

The twenty-seventh day of August

Salah-ud-Din attacked this morning! We had just
set out and the sun was beginning to burn when
suddenly, out of the hills, came a tremendous blar-
ing of horns and screaming. Almost before we could
tighten our ranks a band of horsemen swept down
upon us. The famous Turkish cavalry! The sight
was enough to panic anyone and it certainly
panicked me. My first instinct was to flee, but I was
riding right in the center of the column, just behind
King Richard, and I was surrounded by men. There
was nowhere to go even if I could have figured out
how to make my horse go there.

The attack lasted but a few minutes—it was more
of a skirmish than a battle—then the horsemen
wheeled their mounts around and disappeared back
into the hills. One of the foot soldiers who guard
our left flank was pierced by an arrow, but he
survived. No one was killed. Throughout the day,
however, the attacks became more frequent and we
suffered more casualties. Although those of us who
ride in the center of the column are out of range of
the arrows—the flanking soldiers bear the brunt of
the attacks—my heart still leaped into my throat at

every new onslaught. War is not something one gets used to.

I am beginning to learn a little about the tactics of warfare. The king has organized the knights in three divisions and has protected our left flank with the infantry, both spearmen and bowmen. I can see that this strategy is the most logical. The problem, however, is that we must go at the foot soldiers' pace, which is excruciatingly slow and makes us easy targets for the Turks. It is hard to move along so sluggishly, just waiting for each attack. Because the Turks are on horseback, they use light bows and their arrows cannot pierce through the knights' mail, but they stick in. I saw a knight this morning riding on the left flank who had so many arrows protruding from his armor that he looked like a hedgehog. Unperturbed, however, he simply pulled them out one by one and tossed them to the nearest of our archers. The horses are more vulnerable, however, as they are less well armored. Our archers, not being mounted, carry heavier bows and more powerful arrows, but the Turkish horsemen dart in and out again so quickly they have little time to shoot.

The foot soldiers wear no mail, only thick leather jerkins and tunics. This clothing is heavy enough to deflect most of the Turkish arrows, but the men are still suffering casualties. For this reason the king has divided them into two groups. One group marches on the left and shields us. The other group marches on the right and has an easier time of it, walking beside the baggage train between the knights and the sea. Then the two groups alternate. King

Richard has passed down strict orders that the army is to keep in close formation and ignore all provocations. No one is to break ranks. These are obviously good tactics, but they seem to wear on the men's patience.

The Knights Hospitaler and the Knights Templar are protecting our rear, as these are the soldiers with the most experience of warfare in this country. They are formidable men. I have heard much about them. Both these orders were originally created in connection with the Temple and with the Hospital of St. John in the early days of the Christian Kingdom of Jerusalem. The men who belong to them now, therefore, have been born and brought up in this land and know it well. At first they helped and protected pilgrims. The orders were originally composed of monks who employed knights to guard the travelers, and then the knights themselves joined. Now, I understand, there are practically no monks left within the Knights Hospitaler and Templar at all, and they have become great military armies—the chief fighting force in the Kingdom of Jerusalem, in fact, and the best of all possible fighters. They are haughty and proud men, however, and do not associate over much with the king's regular knights and nobles. Even though they are King Guy's vassals, they will not acknowledge obedience to him, but only to their own Grand Masters.

I must confess I am in awe of them and keep well out of their way. They are not above striking down any unfortunate person who gets in their path.

The twenty-ninth day of August

We have marched past Haifa and over the ridge of
Mount Carmel to Caesarea. The heat is intense and
our heavily armored men are suffering badly. The
horses are not doing well either. They are huge beasts
and not accustomed to this weather. Salah-ud-Din
has been before us wherever we go. All the fortresses
have been burned to the ground and the crops
destroyed. It is fortunate that we have the ships to
supply us. Many men have succumbed to sunstroke,
however, and I am also sick, but not too sick to
perform my duties. Every evening I attend the king
and faithfully record the number of casualties we are
experiencing.

We are to pause here in Caesarea tonight. This
was once a formidable fortress, but now lies in
ruins. It is set amidst high sand dunes studded with
low, scrubby bushes and has a lonely, haunted air to
it. The ground is red and stony, and the stunted
flat-topped trees with gnarled trunks give little
shade.

I walked the old streets for hours after we camped
early this afternoon. The king himself was slightly
wounded by a well-aimed spear and had to rest.

The builders of Caesarea used whatever was at
hand to construct this fortress town and, as it was
once an important Roman city, the Roman ruins
have been assimilated into the Christian fortress.
The streets and walls incorporate many blocks and
columns of Roman marble. It was strange to me to
walk under old arches and see glistening white

pedestals, with Latin inscriptions intact, forming part of the old stone walls on either side of me. As well I saw the remains of an old Roman aqueduct that must once have brought water down from the foothills of the mountains that lie to the north. What a noble people the old Romans must have been. My father told me many tales about them.

The city is in ruins, but the harbor, fortunately for our ships, is still good. The entrance is on the northern side. The Romans planned the harbor this way, I learned, so the sand that is washed along this shore by the currents from the south will not fill it up. I found a small blue glass bottle half buried in the rubble along the water's edge. The glass is delicate and hazy, and the bottle wrought with exceedingly great skill. It is of Roman make, I think, and it seems a miracle that it has not been broken. I tucked it into a pouch at my belt and shall endeavor to keep it safe during this journey.

Walking amongst these ruins has given rise to strange feelings and thoughts within me. The Romans were a powerful and cultured people, so my father said. Toward the close of their time they even renounced their pagan gods and embraced Christianity. Who would ever have thought that their magnificent towns and fortresses would fall into rubble, only to be used to build yet another people's towns and fortresses? And that those in their turn would be destroyed. Where does it end, I wonder?

The thirtieth day of August

Mercadier, the king's lieutenant, came to me this morning with a leather vest, short sword and scabbard.

"The fighting will be more intense now," he said. "The king feels you should be armed. Follow me and I will show you how to use the sword."

The vest is thick and itchy. I cannot move my arms freely. The sword feels awkward hanging by my side in the scabbard and useless in my hand. It is very heavy. Mercadier urged me to swing at him and it took all of my strength to do so. The first time my sword hit his shield, the shock was so great that I was knocked backward off my feet and landed in the dust on my backside. My foot, of course, betrayed me and caused me even more difficulties. To his credit Mercadier did not so much as remark on it, but I do not think I am cut out to be a soldier.

Still, by the end of the morning I was swinging with more control and stayed on my feet most of the time. What it would be like to wield this weapon on horseback I cannot imagine. The thought that I might have to is even more unimaginable. But I might.

The thirty-first day of August

I rode armed today for the first time. It was a seductive experience. Sitting astride a horse with a sword at my side, I was no longer Matthew, the cripple. I was a man of power. It felt good.

The first day of September

The Turkish forces continue to harass us every day. The sun beats down so fiercely, I would be tempted to remove this heavy jerkin were it not for the hail of arrows that descends on us with every attack. I have not yet been hit, although one or two have whistled past uncomfortably close.

Our nerves are stretched to the limit. How long will this go on?

The second day of September

There are rumors that Salah-ud-Din is massing his army for a major attack. I think my horse realizes how anxious I am as it has become very skittish. Tempers are growing short. Fights break out daily over small, unimportant issues. We ride much more quietly now. All the usual good humor and banter are gone. Men sit their horses in grim silence. We are all tormented by the flies. They descend on us in hordes, feeding off our sweat. The fleas in this land seem to have particularly voracious appetites, but perhaps it is only because I cannot scratch beneath this cursed leather jerkin. Hawks circle ominously overhead. The Turks did not attack us today. I would welcome this, except that the king feels it is a sign that Salah-ud-Din is preparing for a major battle.

The fifth day of September

We are approaching a wooded area known as the Forest of Arsuf. We will be crossing through it tomorrow. There is a rumor going around that the forest will be set ablaze by the Turks while we are in it. We have seen no sign at all of Salah-ud-Din's army. My hand shakes as I write this. I think I will dream of fire this night.

The sixth day of September

We crossed through the forest without incident. As we emerged from it the men sent up shouts of relief and good spirits and I joined in most heartily, but our voices died away as we saw what lay on the other side.

We rode out onto a wide plain and there, on the far side of it, was a vast army in battle array. We pulled up in shock and stared. I have never seen such a fearsome sight. For several moments King Richard sat his horse, seemingly immobilized. Then incredibly he broke into a wide smile.

"At last!" he shouted. "At last we will be done with this infernal harassment!" He turned to face his men. "We will have our battle now, my comrades, and the Saracens will know the might of God!"

The cheers broke out again, but this time it was the cry of the crusade.

"God wills it!" the king shouted and "God wills it!" we cried back. For a moment I even forgot my fear, but it has returned. Dear God protect us, it has returned.

The king ordered camp struck on our side of the plain. Only the king's pavilion was erected—the rest of the soldiers slept in their armor, their weapons close at hand. The king gave orders that extra provisions were to be distributed, and everyone feasted well. After the meal I was summoned to King Richard's tent. All of his nobles were there. Duke Hugh of Burgundy stood to one side of King Richard, King Guy of Jerusalem on the other. Conrad of Montserrat sulked in the background. He is still angered over the king's decision that Guy is the rightful king of Jerusalem.

"Write," the king commanded me, and I hastened to set up my inkhorn and parchments on a small table. The king then proceeded to lay out the order of battle for the next day. My hand was shaking again, but I gritted my teeth and forced the trembling to stop.

We are to ride out tomorrow morning in a column with the first light of dawn, straight toward Salah-ud-Din's forces. The Knights Templar will ride at the head of the army, one of the most dangerous positions. Next will come the Bretons and the men of Anjou, King Richard's own men, then King Guy of Jerusalem with the Poitevins. In the fourth division will march the Normans and the English guarding King Richard's dragon standard, and after them the French contingents. In the rear, the other position of greatest danger, will be the Knights Hospitaler.

"We will be under constant attack as soon as we set foot on the plain," the king said, frowning at us all. "But we will not fight back."

Eyebrows rose at this and I was so surprised I stopped writing and stared with the rest. The king glared at me and I bent quickly to my task again.

"We will let them hurl themselves at us until their

horses are exhausted," the king went on. "Then, and only then, will I give the signal for attack. It will be six blasts of a trumpet, two in the van of our column, two in the center and two in the rear. Then, my friends, we will attack, and then Salah-ud-Din will know the full might of a Frankish charge."

There was some murmuring. I heard Duke Hugh mutter that restraining the knights from fighting back would be near impossible, but in the end all the nobles agreed.

But what about me? King Richard had said nothing about me and I wanted to know where I would be placed. As soon as the plans were drawn up, however, the king dismissed me.

"Sire . . ." I stammered, but got no further.

"Off with you, Matthew," he ordered. "I have more business to attend to. This will be a long night."

And a long night it is. I can see the fires of Salah-ud-Din's camp flickering on the other side of the plain. Shadows move back and forth. It seems that no one sleeps there either.

The seventh day of September

I am in such shock that my hand refuses to obey my mind. It spasms and the ink blots the words as I pen them. I must be weeping. Tears are falling upon the parchment and mixing with the ink in rivulets that run off like streams of black blood. I have seen much blood today. I am still stained with it. I cannot write of what has happened. But I must.

Yesterday I sat and stared at the Saracen camp

throughout all the hours of the night. I was not alone. Many of the other soldiers shared my vigil, including one of the Knights Hospitaler. I would have thought him used to battle, but he sat as still and silent and staring as I. We heard the Muslim call to prayer in the darkest hours before the sun began to touch the skies and then a flurry of activity began in the Saracen encampment.

As the sun rose our camp began to come to life as well. The priests said mass. The crusaders—noble knights and soldiers alike—made their confessions, myself among them. Our cooks were serving hot gruel, but I could not eat. All I could do was watch the others and wonder who would be alive after the day and who would be dead. Would I be writing in this journal or lying lifeless on the field of battle?

King Richard emerged from his pavilion. Mercadier shouted orders and the men began to form up, but all in a strange kind of silence. Nowhere did I hear any of the usual bantering and curses. When the whole army was assembled, the king and the duke of Burgundy rode up and down the line, inspecting it and checking the formation. King Richard seemed to be in high good spirits. He shouted to the men, jested, and forced them to respond to him. Slowly I could see the mood changing. By the time he had ridden back and forth twice the men were returning his cheers. Their shoulders straightened, and in the light of the dawning sun I could see blazing eyes and grinning faces. It was an impossible feat, but soon the whole army appeared alive with enthusiasm and impatience. Not a man there seemed to doubt that we would ride over the Saracens and obliterate them. Truly, King Richard is the greatest leader our world has ever known. Finally I was able to catch the king's attention just long enough to ask, "And I, Sire? Where should I ride?"

The question must have caught him off guard. Clearly he hadn't given me a thought. He hesitated for a moment, then said quickly, "With the standard bearers, boy. They will be well protected. Ride with them."

That suited me not at all. In my ignorance I was as caught up in the battle fever as the rest, my fears totally forgotten. I determined that I would not be so far back. The king paid me no further attention and when he took his place at the head of the nobles I maneuvered my horse into the crowd behind him. Mercadier saw me and frowned, but there was no time to do anything about it.

The foot soldiers arrayed themselves on either side of us, a command rang out and the column began to move. Across the plain the Turkish army waited.

We marched at a steady pace. We reached the halfway mark, but still the Turkish army made no move. I kept my hand on the pommel of my sword. It gave me reassurance. It also gave me something to hang onto. My false bravado was ebbing quickly.

Then suddenly the Saracens attacked.

A blare of trumpets shattered the air. Drums and tambourines blasted out. Salah-ud-Din's army surged forward in a screaming wave of brilliant color. Pennons, flags and banners streamed above them.

As they closed in upon us our infantry greeted them with a barrage of spears and arrows, but the Turkish army seemed to be everywhere. I saw long-robed men of the desert amongst their troops. I had seen them before and marveled at their horseman-ship. Then I saw men with skin so dark it was almost black. Nubians, they are called. I have heard of such people, but never before seen them. The Turkish archers swept by and a rain of arrows flew at us so thickly that for a moment the hard bright-ness of the sun was dimmed. The Saracen forces attacked, then wheeled around and attacked again. We marched grimly forward. The sun rose and passed its zenith. The Saracens attacked and attacked yet again. The Master of the Hospitalers rode up to the front, his horse in a frenzy of sweat. The Hospitalers in the rear were bearing the brunt of the strikes and he begged the king to give permis-sion to charge. King Richard refused, even though it was plain that we were losing men and horses at an alarming rate. The heat was almost unbearable. The noise of the Turkish drums and cymbals was driving us mad.

The assaults continued. Several more of the nobles spurred their horses forward to beg the king to give the signal to attack, but still he refused. He rode on, his jaw set. I saw King Guy plead with him, but all the king of Jerusalem got was a curt shake of the head. Around me men were cursing and swearing with every arrow that fell.

Then a commotion broke out in our rear. The king turned to see what was happening, but before he could shout out a command to stop them, the Marshal of the Order of Hospitalers and another knight broke ranks and charged the Turks. At once the rest of the Hospitalers and the French knights galloped after them.

"God's legs!" King Richard cursed as we saw our own infantry being run down in the attack, but it was too late. He could do nothing to stop it. He shouted out an order for the general assault to be sounded and then stormed after them. The whole Frankish army galloped after him and I was swept along.

I must stop here for a while. My mind is overwhelmed with memories and I cannot control my tears.

Later . . .

I am tempted not to continue with this account. It is almost as if by not writing down what happened, I can deny that it did. But I will go on. I have stopped weeping and my hand, strangely enough, does not shake anymore. It is as steady as a dead man's. Perhaps I am a dead man—inside.

I saw and heard the Frankish knights charging on their huge warhorses, spears leveled. The pounding of the horses' hooves was so great it drowned out all else. Such a charge is an awesome sight. No matter how often I watched it in practice, it never ceased to astound me. I cannot imagine what it would be like to have such a wall of enormous, powerful beasts thundering toward me, with knights riding shield to shield, their lances lowered.

King Richard rode at their head, brandishing his

sword high. I saw the flicker of his blade cut in every direction. He tore into the Turkish soldiers like a man possessed by the devil. Everywhere around him I saw men fall. He carved a path through that army like a reaper mowing hay with his sickle.

The Turkish lines broke. Then they reformed, and the world around me turned into a screaming inferno.

I have no memory of drawing my sword, but I found myself swinging it wildly as a Turkish soldier galloped past me. Then I swung again as yet another man came at me from the side. I think I might have struck him, I do not know. In my terror I struck out blindly. I felt a sudden stinging in my shoulder and was amazed to see blood flowing from it. I had not even seen my attacker. I swung again and again. My horse was neighing with fear under me. The poor mare is not a warhorse and was as panicked as I. Time seemed to stretch out. I felt as if I had been in the midst of that noise and insanity for most of my life. I fought with an intensity and desperation that I didn't know I possessed. I think I wounded several men. I may have killed some—I will never know.

A Turkish noble, turbaned and robed in flowing, flaming scarlet, stormed straight at me. His sword was raised high. I swung to meet his charge and then my eyes met his. It was Rashid! I choked back a cry as I saw what was in those eyes. It was pure hatred. Rashid had not forgiven me.

My sword arm dropped. I could not move. As if in a trance I watched him come at me and I knew he would kill me. Knew he had to kill me. How else could he purge his shame? The blade of his sword flashed once in the sun. It began to sweep down. It seemed to move with a swimming slowness.

Another blade streaked across. It knocked Rashid's weapon aside and then buried itself in his chest. I had only time enough to see the look in his eyes change—almost, it seemed, to relief—and then he fell.

Beside me Mercadier wrenched his blade out of Rashid's body even as he hauled his horse around to parry yet another blow.

I must have continued fighting—I did survive—but I have no memory of the battle from the time I saw Rashid fall until later when it was all over. I returned to my senses to find Mercadier himself binding my wound. I shook him off and staggered back to my tent. I sat outside it for a long while. The moon rose and bathed the field in a silver brilliance. I could see the bodies strewn across the plain. The priests had said mass over the Christians and given last rites wherever possible. The vultures had come. It had been a great victory for us, Mercadier had said, exulting.

Already many of our soldiers were scavenging among the dead, seeking plunder and souvenirs. I got to my feet and limped out. I searched for most of the night, but I could not find Rashid's body. He is dead though. I know it.

How would I have felt if it had been Rashid who had urged me to flee and I who had escaped the massacre of my comrades? Guilty, I am certain.

And I would have blamed Rashid too for being the cause of it. Perhaps that is not sensible, but it is the way men feel. Would I have blamed him enough, hated him enough to kill him? I do not suppose I will ever know. But I do know that I mourn his loss. The one person in all my life whom I could have called friend. And now he is gone.

The eighth day of September

The king called me to his pavilion early this morning.

"You were in the thick of it, Matthew my lad," he said. "Good boy! And I hear you acquitted yourself well for a scribe. I'm pleased with you." He held out a ring to me—a golden ring with a dark red stone that glistened with a fire of its own.

I stood stupidly, looking at it.

"Take it, my lad. You've earned it," the king urged.

I did not want it, but no one refuses a king's gift. I reached for it. He dropped it into my palm. It burned. I felt as if it were searing deep into my flesh.

"You will write an account of our victory," the king said. "Spare no details. You were there yourself, so you will be able to describe how valiantly we fought, how glorious was our victory. This is a tale that will be told over and over, Matthew. Write it with every bit of skill you possess."

"Everything, Sire?" I asked.

"Of course. Everything."

"Even the looting of the dead by our soldiers?"

For a second the king's brows furrowed. He

looked at me as if puzzled. "If you wish, my lad. But that's not important. It is but a normal part of war."

We struck camp soon after and have been marching southward all day. There has been no sign of Salah-ud-Din's army. Our victory has been complete indeed. I have written faithfully of the battle and spared no words in describing the bravery of the king and his knights.

I wrote as well of the bodies that we left behind, Muslim and Christian, sprawled out together in death. Those who read my story will read of that as well.

I hid the ring in the bottom of my pouch. I do not wish to look at it.

The tenth day of September

We have reached the port of Jaffa. From here we must turn inland to follow the road to Jerusalem.

As we drew near to the city we could see that the walls lay in ruins. At first there was general jubilation at the sight, but it quickly turned to dismay. There are no Turkish forces left in Jaffa and Salah-ud-Din made certain to destroy it to such an extent that we will not be able to lodge within the town. We are camped instead just outside the walls. The general feeling in the camp is that we should press on and march directly to Jerusalem, but the king has determined that our army must rest first. I can see the wisdom of his decision, but I know also, from listening in to the council meeting last night, that King Richard is worried about leaving the coast. We will no longer have the support and protection of our ships. If Salah-ud-Din managed to cut off our supply line from the coast entirely as we marched inland we would be in trouble.

I find that I cannot bring myself to worry, like the king, or to rejoice, like the rest of our crusaders. It is as if a hand has reached inside me and turned off all feeling.

The twentieth day of September

We are rebuilding Jaffa. I report to the king each morning and do what is required of me, then I wander. Most of my wanderings take me along the shore. It is, I suppose, a beautiful place, but I can no longer see beauty.

The thirtieth day of September

Now that the city is somewhat restored, the king has brought Queen Berengaria and Queen Joanna down. Yusra is probably with them. I wonder how she fares. I should ask after her, but even thinking of her brings the memory of Rashid rushing back so forcefully that I cannot bear it.

The first day of October

"With God's grace we hope to recover the city of Jerusalem and the Holy Sepulcher by twenty days after Christmas and then return to our own dominions."

So wrote King Richard to the Pope last night. It sounds so simple and so hopeful. So why do the lines in his face deepen by the day and his eyes grow harder?

The tenth day of October

Today King Richard sent a missive to Salah-ud-Din. I wrote it. After all the usual salutations and compliments, it read as follows.

"The Muslims and the Franks are bleeding to death, the country is utterly ruined, and goods and lives have been sacrificed on both sides. The time has come to stop this. Jerusalem is for us an object of worship that we could not give up even if there were only one of us left."

He went on to demand the surrender of Jerusalem to our forces and the return of the True Cross. We await Salah-ud-Din's reply.

The thirteenth day of October

Salah-ud-Din has sent his reply under a flag of truce with his brother, al-Adil Saif-ud-Din. King Richard seems to like this man very much, and he is indeed impressive. He has about him an air of quiet concentration. The answer he bore, however, was not to our king's liking.

"Jerusalem is as much ours as yours," Salah-ud-Din wrote in his reply. "Indeed, it is even more sacred to us than it is to you, for it is the place from which our Prophet Muhammad, God's peace and blessing be upon him, made his ascent into heaven and the place where our community will gather on the day of Judgement. Do not imagine that we can renounce it." He also refused to return the True Cross, saying that it will be useful for further bartering.

The furrows in my king's brow grow deeper.

The fifteenth day of October

As I write this I can still hear Queen Joanna berating King Richard at the top of her lungs. How can a king be so brave and noble and yet at the same time so witless?

He has put forward the most startling of peace proposals. It is this: that if Salah-ud-Din would grant Palestine to his brother al-Adil Saif-ud-Din, then he, Richard of England, would arrange for al-Adil Saif-ud-Din to marry Queen Joanna. As a dowry he would give her the coastal cities from Acre to Ascalon. They could live at Jerusalem and all Christians would be given free access to the city.

I myself wrote up this proposal. The most surprising news is that Salah-ud-Din has accepted it! Perhaps he thinks King Richard is joking.

Queen Joanna most certainly does not, however. She is in a towering rage and I believe she even threw things at the king when he told her of the plan. Obviously, this is not the solution.

The thirty-first day of October

We are on the march, heading for Jerusalem. The soldiers sing and cheer and are in the best of spirits. The pilgrims pray and weep with joy. Everyone thinks that Jerusalem will be ours within the month. The temperature is cooler and walking is easier.

I did not see Yusra before we left. She and the two queens stayed behind in Jaffa. I wish now I had.

The fifth day of November

Our advance has slowed. The road begins to rise

and the path is more difficult, but it is not just the journey that impedes us. Salah-ud-Din has destroyed all before us and the king is determined to rebuild as much as we can along the way. This is a Christian pilgrims' route and he has resolved to restore the castles. The Saracens harass us but only lightly, usually by sending out patrols to raid our lines of communication and to attack any foraging parties that are not well guarded. Salah-ud-Din is biding his time and waiting for us.

This king of ours is indeed brave and a man of honor. The count of St. Pol was leading one such party and yesterday we received a desperate message from him saying he was outnumbered and surrounded by the Turkish forces. The king immediately sent the earl of Leicester to reinforce the count's band and then determined to follow them himself. Calling me to him he set off at a gallop with Mercadier and a band of his most trusted soldiers. I galloped behind, hanging grimly onto the saddle. My horsemanship has improved immensely, but I part company more often than not with my horse at anything more than a trot.

We arrived at a place where we could see what was happening. The Frankish soldiers, the earl of Leicester and his men included, were totally surrounded. The Turks were circling them and firing arrows into their midst with deadly accuracy. The Christians were greatly outnumbered. Even as we watched two horses fell and their riders tumbled motionless to the ground.

The king made as if to spur his horse forward, but Mercadier was quick to lay a hand on his arm.

"You will not succeed in rescuing them, Sire. It is better that they die alone than that you risk death in this attack and so endanger the whole crusade."

The king turned to face him, his face frightening in its anger.

"I sent those men there. If they die without me, may I never again be called king!" he shouted.

With a quick gesture to his men, a curt command to me to hold my place and a wild war cry he charged forward, sword flashing in the sun.

The intensity and unexpectedness of his charge turned the battle and in a few moments it was over. Those Turks who were not cut down turned and ran. In celebration King Richard's men carried on their spear-points the heads of those slain back to our crusaders. The victory was a great boost to the morale of all the army.

But was Mercadier the wiser? What if the king had been slain? He is the only real leader here. What would have happened to the crusade then? King Richard is undoubtedly a soldier courageous beyond words, but does he have the right to take such risks?

The twenty-second day of November

We are deep inland now. The green of the coastal trees and shrubs is giving way to reddish-colored earth and stone-covered hills. The horses' hooves slip on the rocks and the men on foot curse the treacherousness of the path. It has been raining steadily for the past two days and is growing colder.

Today we reached a small town called Ramleh. There had been a Christian church here, but the Turks burned it down many years ago during the time of the great Duke Godfrey of Bouillon's crusade, one of the Knights Hospitaler told me. I stumbled onto the ruins during one of my wanderings, last night at dusk. I did not explore very much as the place seemed full of ghosts. It is a sad town.

This knight is different from most of them. His name is Arnald and he is friendly to me. It was he whom I saw sitting and watching the Saracen camp the night before our battle. This morning as I was resting under a large tree, sheltering from the rain, he came to sit beside me and began talking. He was born in Jerusalem and is descended from a knight who rode with Godfrey of Bouillon and then settled in Jerusalem after the city was retaken. Stories of that crusade have been passed down in his family and he recounted some of them to me.

As we talked my hand found something smooth in the grass. I rubbed it absentmindedly, thinking it was a stone. Then I took a closer look and realized it was the skull of some animal. I do not know why, but it intrigued me. I began to dig away the earth that partially concealed it. When Arnald saw what I was doing he bent to help me. After a time we unearthed the skull of a horse. But what a huge skull! Our warhorses are of a great size, but this one must have been one of the biggest ever bred. It could not have been a Turkish horse for they are mere ponies and much smaller.

"Do you think this could have been a crusader warhorse?" I asked Arnald.

"Most assuredly it was," he answered. Then his face grew thoughtful. He hoisted the skull up and stared at it.

"Duke Godfrey's crusaders came by here," he said. "They came through Ramleh even as we are doing. They had to, to get to Jerusalem. There is a story told in my family about my great-grandfather. He was a young knight then, named Theobald. In the service of the Duke of Bouillon he was, and he had a warhorse of immense size and fame. Even the name of that horse has been passed down in the old stories. It was called Centurion. That destrier was the only horse to survive the long, hard trek from the forests of the Ardennes to the Holy Land, but it did finally die. And it died right here at Ramleh, if my memory serves me rightly."

I stared at the skull. "Could this be . . . ?"

Arnald rubbed his hand the length of it with a tenderness I had not expected of him. "It might, lad," he said. "It might well be."

The twelfth day of December

The weather continues to be dreadful. It rains and it rains and it rains. It is so cold that we have even had storms of frozen ice pellets. My head and arms are bruised from them. The mud is everywhere. Yesterday the king's groom's horse slipped and broke its leg. It had to be killed. I cannot remember when I last had a hot broth. As we venture further up into the hills the trees become sparse, so we can find little

wood for fire. What we can find is wet and hard to
kindle. My clothes are soaking wet and do not dry
out overnight as my tent leaks copiously. Even the
knights' armor is beginning to rust. I have a cough
that gives me no rest and I shiver constantly.

The fifteenth day of December

We have reached a town called Latroun. The king
has decreed that we shall stay here to celebrate the
Yuletide festivities. In spite of all the discomfort, the
soldiers are in a jubilant mood. The priests are also
happy because they look forward to celebrating
mass in the Holy City within the month. The king
promised we would be in Jerusalem twenty days
after Yuletide and they are counting on that.

Not everyone is so optimistic, however. I have
talked much with Arnald these past few days. He
and the other Knights Hospitaler and Templar
know this country far better than we do and their
outlook is glum.

"If we lay siege to the city the Saracen forces will
come up from behind. It will be like Acre all over
again, but our access to the sea will be cut off and
we will not have ships supplying us and supporting
us as we did there. We will be caught between the
garrison defending Jerusalem and the army
surrounding us," Arnald explained to me. "And
suppose the king does capture Jerusalem," he went
on. "What then? How will he hold it? The pilgrims
amongst us will make their vows at the Holy
Sepulcher and then, their pilgrimage completed,
go home. Many of the soldiers will probably leave

as well. We will be alone, outnumbered and without any means of renewing our supplies."

The rest of the camp does not want to hear this kind of talk, however, so the knights just mutter amongst themselves.

I think I must have a fever. I burn hot and then succumb to chills that rack my body. I am glad we will be resting here for a while.

The first day of January, the year of our Lord, 1192

A new year. What will it bring? We are are on the march again. I am so ill I can barely stay on my horse. The mud is so thick the poor beast can hardly wade through it. I feel for the pilgrims trying to make their way on foot. The conditions are terrible and there is sickness throughout the party. Many are dying. I fear our way will be marked for future wayfarers by the number of crosses we leave behind us.

The fifth day of January

We have reached Beit Nuba. We are almost within sight of Jerusalem, but the king is in a terrible mood. He has been conferring every night with his nobles and with the Knights Hospitaler and Templar. He has called for a council meeting tonight. I am to attend and record it. I do not know how I will write. My vision blurs and my hand shakes so that I can hardly hold a quill. My head hurts most dreadfully. When I cough the pain in my chest doubles me over. If only I could get dry and warm!

The sixth day of January

The decision has been made. We will not lay siege to
Jerusalem. We will retreat. I cannot imagine how the
soldiers and the pilgrims will feel about this news.
To be so close!

I have been lying in my tent ever since coming
back from the council meeting last night. I am
trying to write curled up in a pool of freezing mud.
The wick is sputtering and about to go out. My
whole body feels as if it is on fire. It is almost too
painful to breathe. I think if I have one more
coughing spell it will kill me. My head is swimming
and my eyes struggle to focus. I cannot see to write.
I must stop.

I cannot believe this is how our glorious crusade
is to end. In misery, mud and despair . . .

✝   ✝   ✝

The thirtieth day of March

Over two months since I have written in this journal. Much has happened. First of all, I nearly died.

When I unrolled my parchment this morning
after such a long time I could barely remember writing the last entry. I was so overcome with fever,
illness and despair that night, all was vague and
uncertain. They tell me I was found shaking and
witless the next morning. Somehow or other I was
bundled up, slung over my faithful horse and
brought back to Jaffa. I remember nothing of it.
Indeed, I remember nothing until last week when I
opened my eyes to find myself in an unfamiliar

room with Yusra, of all people, caring for me. I have been sliding in and out of death's grasp for weeks, it seems. Today I am hungry, so perhaps I will live after all.

I am too weak to write more. I will continue tomorrow.

The first day of April

I was unable to write yesterday. Today I feel a little stronger. I must continue with my journal now that I have taken it up again. It is the only way I can bring some kind of sense and order to what has happened.

As I have recorded I have no remembrance of the retreat from Jerusalem back to Jaffa. When I came to myself a few days ago I opened my eyes to see a whitewashed room filled with sunlight. It was so bright, in fact, that I had to close my eyes again immediately against the pain of it. I think I probably lapsed back into unconsciousness then. The next time I awoke it was evening and the light was softer. A breeze wafted in through a window on one side of me, bringing with it the sweet scent of flowers and oranges, and I could hear the murmur of the ocean.

The first thing that impressed itself upon me was the deep, delicious comfort of the bed on which I lay. It was piled with pillows. I could feel the softness of silk against my cheek. There was a smell of incense in the room. For a moment I was back in Rashid's tent, but with that memory came a stab of pain and I thrust it away quickly.

"Are you awake, Matthew?"

The voice seemed to come out of thin air. Then I turned my head and to my amazement saw Yusra kneeling on the carpet beside my bed. She was dressed in a soft, light-colored shift and her head was covered with a scarf. She looked different. Older.

I tried to sit up, but fell back as the room swirled and dipped around me.

"Lie still, Matthew," Yusra said. "You are too weak to get up." There was an authority in her voice that I had not heard before.

"Where am I?" I managed to ask.

"In Jaffa. In Queen Joanna's house. When they brought you back the king ordered that you be brought here and cared for by his own healer. It seems he thinks highly of you."

"And you . . . ?"

She sensed what I was trying to ask.

"I serve the queen. As always. She asked me to oversee your recovery. I have learned a few words in her language and I am more obedient now, so she rewards me with fine clothes and even a few jewels."

Her voice was flat, her face carefully expressionless. I stared at her. This was not the Yusra I remembered. It was not just that she seemed older—there was something else hiding behind her eyes.

"Are you happy now?" I asked. It was a stupid question, but I make the excuse that I was not yet thinking properly.

She smiled, a small rueful smile that ended with a downward twist to her mouth.

"I have brought you fruit, Matthew. Eat what you can. You must regain your strength," she said.

She served me and would not look at me again, nor answer any more questions.

She has come to sit with me every day since then. When I asked for my quills and writing materials to be brought to me she was eager to do so.

"It is good, Matthew, that you write again. A scribe is an honored person. You should be working," she told me.

Her words were so like Rashid's that again his memory flooded my mind with pain.

Whenever I ask Yusra about herself, however, she turns from me and avoids the question.

The third day of April

To my surprise Queen Joanna came in to see me this morning. She said the king had sent to know how I was faring and she wanted to see for herself. I tried to get up when she entered the room, but between my weakness and my cursed foot I fell flat on my face. Then, of course, all was concern and commiseration as the servants helped me back onto the bed. I felt like a fool.

I was burning to know what had happened during all the long weeks that I was ill, however, and after I had reassured Her Grace ten times that I was feeling strong enough, she gave me the latest tidings. At first she did not want to talk overmuch so as not to tire me, but when she saw that I was becoming feverish again with the frustration of not knowing, she humored me.

King Richard is away, she told me, rebuilding the fortress city of Ascalon. That city stands on the caravan route between Egypt and Syria and is an important stronghold. Negotiations with Salah-ud-Din are still going on. Rumors abound as to what the king's plans are, but no one here seems to know for certain. The council has now overturned the king's earlier decision and declared Conrad of Montferrat king of Jerusalem, but in the light of our failure that announcement seems laughable to me. King Conrad is urging another march on the Holy City and the majority of the crusaders back him, so the gossip goes.

The sixteenth day of April

I am on the mend with a vengeance now. The king is due back next week and I intend to greet him on my feet and ready in all ways to get back to work.

Yusra brings me everything that I need and is often at my bedside when I wake. I find her quiet presence comforting, but I sense that she is hiding some trouble. She is not happy, not content, but she will not tell me what is wrong. I am determined to break through to her and find out.

The twentieth day of April

Finally I have been able to talk with Yusra, but now I am more worried than ever. She came in with Queen Joanna early this morning. It pleased me to see that I am strong enough now to make a proper obeisance to Her Grace. King Richard will be returning soon, she said, and my heart leaped with gladness when she added that he hoped I would be well enough to resume my duties with him then. I most certainly will.

When the queen left, Yusra stayed behind to collect some dishes. Her eyes were red and it looked as if she had been weeping.

"Is aught wrong?" I asked, but she just shook her head.

"You've been weeping," I persisted.

"I have not," she replied.

"You have," I insisted.

When she made as if to leave the room I took a step forward and grasped her by the arm.

"I saved your life, Yusra," I said as gently as I could. "I am responsible for you, remember? Surely, you can talk with me?"

At that, to my horror, she covered her face with her hands and broke into sobs. I looked around quickly, but the queen was well away and no servants were within earshot. I pulled Yusra toward a low couch in the corner of the room and sat down with her. I patted her back awkwardly. I made small noises intended to be comforting, but I think I sounded more like a goat in distress. Finally she wiped the back of her hand across her eyes, hiccuped once or twice and then looked at me.

"What is it?" I asked. "Do they not treat you well here?"

"They treat me exceedingly well," she answered, her voice trembling and the words so muffled I could barely understand her. "The queen is kindness itself now that I have agreed to obey her every wish."

"Then what is amiss?" I persisted, confused.

She took a deep breath and got her voice back under control. "You do not understand, Matthew. No one understands. I cannot live here. I am Muslim. And I am no longer a child. I am growing into a woman and there are customs I must observe, things I must do. I must be with my own people. I cannot stay here." She drew the shawl she wore closer around her head. "I must dress like a Muslim woman. Obey the Muslim laws. I cannot do that here."

I bit my lip. "Is there no way you can compromise? After all, you found a way to pray here."

"They discovered what I was doing and made me stop," she replied. "Father Aimar and the queen are determined that I shall embrace your faith. I have even pretended to do so out of fear of them. My faith allows me to do that, to pretend, but in my heart I am dying with the shame of it. I cannot keep on like this. Would you abandon your God, Matthew?"

What answer could I give to that? Of course I would not abandon my God. But if the Muslim God, the Christian God and the Jewish God are the same, as Rashid believed, why could this stubborn girl not worship in our way?

I know the answer in my heart, but I do not want to listen to it. Rashid would never have forsworn his faith and neither would I. Why should Yusra be asked to?

The twenty-second day of April

King Richard has returned. He has set up camp just outside the remains of the city walls. He summoned me to his tent last evening and I went armed with my writing materials. There followed a council meeting that lasted well into the night. I am weak with weariness, but exhilarated as well. I am working again.

There was much to discuss. Disturbing news has come from England. It seems that the king's younger brother, Prince John, has been fomenting trouble. There has never been any love lost between those two and the news is that Prince John is forging an alliance with King Philip. This cannot bode well for King Richard, but what can he do? He cannot abandon the crusade now.

The twenty-eighth day of April

More bad news. King Conrad has been murdered! Rumors are flying all around. Some people even have the temerity to suggest that it was done at King Richard's orders. Others believe it more likely that he was killed by Assassins, a band of heretic Muslims who hide out in the mountains and strike at crusaders whenever they can. In any case the situation here is in chaos. Does this mean that Guy is king of Jerusalem again? No one seems to know.

The fifth day of May

These lords and princes do seem to have their own standards of conduct. King Conrad's widow, Queen Isabella, who is still queen of Jerusalem, has married Count Henry of Champagne. There was certainly no time wasted there! Count Henry is a nephew of King Richard's, so now King Richard is supporting his claim to the kingdom of Jerusalem through Henry's wife, the queen. My head swims with this nonsense. I write it all down faithfully for King Richard, then come here and record my disgust in my private journal. Blessed journal. What would I do without it?

The twenty-ninth day of May

King Richard is keeping me busy writing letters. There is yet more disquieting news from England. The conspiracy between Prince John and King Philip deepens. The prince seems to be lusting after the English crown, and King Philip—although he swore an oath that he would not do so—is readying himself to attack King Richard's Angevin empire in the Frankish lands. My king is in a foul temper. I know he is tempted to abandon the crusade and return to save his kingdoms. The other nobles and princes will not hear of it, however.

The thirtieth day of May

The council members met last night and decided that whatever King Richard did, they would attack Jerusalem. The king listened to this ultimatum like a man of stone. My fingers trembled as I wrote. The news was somehow leaked to the soldiers and they, with the exception of the Knights Hospitaler and Templar, of course, are celebrating. As I write this I can hear the men dancing and singing. King

Richard stormed out of the meeting without a word and has secluded himself in his tent.

How does anyone think that this foray on Jerusalem will be any different from the last? Nothing has changed, except that Salah-ud-Din has had the winter to strengthen his walls and fortifications.

The second day of June

King Richard remains secluded in his tent. Meanwhile, the army prepares to march. The king faces a terrible decision. If he stays to lead the army and by some chance does succeed in taking and holding Jerusalem, he will be the most powerful king in Europe and no one will be able to stand against him—not even his cowardly brother, Prince John, or that deceitful traitor, King Philip. He will be the conqueror who restored the Holy City to Christendom. But suppose he fails again and by trying returns to England too late to save his kingdom. What then? I feel for him. Thank God I am not a king and I do not have to make such fateful decisions.

The fifth day of June

Finally King Richard emerged. He called another council meeting this morning. He has made his decision—he will lead the crusade on Jerusalem. He has pledged himself to stay in Palestine until next Easter. As he made the pronouncement his voice shook. The choice must have cost him dearly.

The advance on Jerusalem is underway. Again.

The sixth day of June

We marched at dawn today. Having decided to lay siege to Jerusalem the king seems a changed man. Once more he rides along the line of his soldiers, exhorting them and filling all with enthusiasm. Once more he leads them in their battlecry of "God wills it!"

He seems to have cast aside all doubts and has determined that this time he will be successful. So confident is he now that he is allowing Queen Joanna to accompany us. He made the offer to Queen Berengaria as well, but she refused. Queen Joanna, however, is delighted with the adventure.

King Richard is of so mercurial a temperament that he can convince himself of whatever he wants, it seems. This troubles me, I must confess, if only to these parchments.

Yusra has not tended to me since I became well and I do not see overly much of her, but she will accompany Queen Joanna, I hear. I have not forgotten my last conversation with her. Events have crowded in to push it out of my mind, but I have not forgotten. How I will help her I do not know, but help her I must. When I see her following the queen about, her face looks more and more sad.

The eleventh day of June

We have reached Beit Nuba again. My memories of this place are not good and I like it no more this time than last. Instead of being cold and miserable, the weather now is so hot that it fairly fries the brain.

Before I was constantly soaked with rain, now I am continuously drenched in sweat.

King Richard has decreed that we will wait here for reinforcements to come from Acre under the command of Count Henry of Champagne. Or should I now refer to him as King Henry? Truth, I do not know and care less. There were no attacks on us along the way. Our only losses were two soldiers who died of snake bite. Salah-ud-Din, it would appear, has withdrawn all his forces into Jerusalem and waits for us there.

The twelfth day of June

My birth day again. I am seventeen years of age now. It has been over a year since we left Messina, my home. I was so desperate to leave, to seek new adventures. Well, I have certainly had them and I am weary. I feel older than my seventeen years. How much longer will it be before I return? Will I ever return?

The twentieth day of June

And still we wait. The soldiers are getting restless. This morning the king sent for me.

"I am going on a foraging patrol, Matthew," he said. "I must have some action. Would you come with me?"

"Most gladly, Sire," I replied and limped as quickly as I could to ready my horse.

We met a small party of Turkish horsemen as we rode closer to Jerusalem and they let loose a few arrows at us, but when our soldiers returned the fire they wheeled and galloped off. Then we found ourselves on top of the hill that is called Montjoie, the hill of joy. There, for the first time, we could actually look down upon the Holy City itself. I was first up onto the brow of the hill. I reined my horse in and drank in the sight. Jerusalem!

The city slumbered, deceptively peaceful behind its massive walls. From this height I could look down on it all. Turrets and minarets sizzled and shone in the heat of the noonday sun. I saw a huge golden dome that I knew had to be the Holy Sepulcher itself, one of the holiest churches in all Christendom. I cannot describe the feelings that fought within me. To look upon Jerusalem! To think that we might retake it—that I might really walk its streets.

And then to think that we probably will not. And if we turn back this time I know I will never look upon it again. Our crusade will have failed. How could I bear that?

As I watched, the party of horsemen that had attacked us galloped up to a gate. It swung open to receive them, then closed again. We are so close!

At that moment the king rode up beside me. I heard him draw in his breath. Then, to my horror, I heard a sob. I stared at him in shock. He was weeping!

He raised his shield to cover his eyes. "I beg God not to let me look upon this city if I cannot deliver it," he said. The words were so muffled I could barely hear them. Then he wrenched cruelly at his destrier's mouth—the only time I have ever seen him do so—and galloped back down the hill, away from the sight of Jerusalem.

I do not know for how long I continued to sit there, staring at the city.

The twenty-fifth day of June

Our soldiers made a successful raid on a rich caravan today and captured much booty.

The twenty-ninth day of June

Count Henry of Champagne—I refuse to call him king and no one else seems to do so either—arrived today with reinforcements. At first there was general rejoicing, but the celebration soon turned sour as scouts returned to say that the sultan had blocked up all the wells between here and Jerusalem. The summer heat rages and now we will have no water. Scouts also report that Salah-ud-Din has mustered an even larger army, which is waiting for us to attack Jerusalem so that it can cut off our supply line from the coast. The situation looks hopeless. A council meeting has been called for tonight.

Later . . .

We are to withdraw. King Richard looks stricken. I had never thought I would feel so much pity for a king.

The thirtieth day of June

Plans are being made to retreat. There is a desolate, defeated air to the whole camp. I must admit that I share it. Then I saw Yusra today and I was shocked at her appearance. She is thin and sickly looking. I called to her, but she would not look in my direction. This problem is serious and I must do something, but what?

The first day of July (early morning)

I lay awake all night. The beginnings of a plan are forming in my mind. I am trying to sort them out. I must do something for Yusra before we retreat—if she journeys to the Frankish lands with Queen Joanna she will never see her own people again.

Later . . .

I presented myself to Queen Joanna after the priests had said mass and we had broken our fast this morning. I asked her if Yusra could come and help me pack up my tent. She looked surprised, as well she might. I have so few possessions, I certainly need no assistance in stowing them away for travel.

She smiled, a kindly but knowing smile. I think perhaps she imagines that I have grown fond of the girl. In her mind that would solve the problem of Yusra very well. Marry her off to me and forget all this nonsense of her needing to be with her own people. The queen, of course, refused to marry a Muslim, but what would it matter for me, a low-born scribe?

If only the solution were that simple. Of course I am fond of the child, but certainly not in that way. When she came out of the queen's pavilion and walked beside me to my own tent, however, I could not help but notice how graceful she is. Her face, framed by her shawl, is beautiful. To my surprise I felt an unfamiliar pang reach in and twist my heart. I am feeling it now, even as I write. I call her a child, but truly she is no longer that. She is a young woman . . .

Enough of such meanderings.

Once inside my tent I invited Yusra to sit down.

"I did not call you here to help me," I said. "I do not need help. It was for something else that I wanted you here."

For a moment she looked at me in alarm. I hastened to reassure her.

"I needed to talk to you," I blurted out. I cannot for the life of me imagine why, but my tongue suddenly felt as thick as a horse's blanket. "I have a plan," I went on, "to return you to your own people."

She stared at me.

I hurried to tell her what had been boiling in my mind. As I spoke I saw her eyes brighten and color come back to her cheeks.

"It may not work," I warned her.

"It will," she answered, her voice fierce. "It *will!*"

So now I am back here in my own tent, contemplating treason to my king yet again. The first time I did so had disastrous results and did no good in the end. I did not save Rashid—only gained his enmity and caused him to feel he had lost his honor. Will trying to help Yusra be just as futile?

I *could* marry her. Force her to convert to Christianity. Our priests would say that is the only way her soul can be saved.

And the thought is not unappealing.

But she will never be happy living with Christians. She would be desolate.

I am beginning to realize that it is not only kings who are faced with terrible decisions.

The third day of July

It is done. How do I feel? I wish I knew. I have never been so confused and so unhappy. It is possible that I have made the biggest mistake of my life.

This is what happened.

I arranged with Yusra to be outside the pavilion she shares with Queen Joanna just after midnight last night, when we could be certain that all the camp had settled for sleep. She did not anticipate any trouble sneaking out as she is not so heavily guarded here as in the city. After all, the thinking was, where could she go? In any case the queen trusts her now and does not worry about the possibility of her escaping any longer.

I hid myself in the bushes and prepared to wait for as long as necessary, but Yusra slipped out very soon after. She stood outside the pavilion, looking around her, and I whistled softly. I knew that the guard who was supposed to be on duty was in the cook's tent drinking up the last of the evening's mead. I had earlier ascertained this was his habit. The camp as a whole is well guarded and there is no apparent danger of a night attack from Salah-ud-Din's forces, so some of our security measures have become very lax.

Yusra heard my whistle and crept into the bushes

beside me. In the moonlight her dark eyes glittered. It could have been with fear, but I think it was more excitement. I prayed that my plan would not fail. I did not want to think of the consequences for her or for me if we were caught.

I had made a reconnaissance the night before and knew where all the guards were positioned. Again, they were not expecting danger during the night. Besides, they were certainly not on the lookout for anyone trying to sneak *out* of the camp.

"Be as quiet as you can," I whispered, and took her by the hand. Then I realized she carried nothing with her.

"Do you not have a bundle?" I asked.

"No," she whispered back. "There is nothing that is mine."

"But you said the queen gave you clothes, jewels . . ." I paused, uncertain.

"They were not mine. I would not take them," she said.

"But the jewels at least!" I urged her. "You could trade them for things that you will need."

"That would be stealing!" She shook her head with a trace of anger. "I've told you, Matthew, the Muslim people take care of their own."

Her voice had begun to rise.

"Hush!" I hissed. "Very well. I believe you." But I could not help thinking that a jewel or two would not have been amiss.

We crept in silence to the perimeter of the camp. I motioned to Yusra to stay where she was for a few moments while I made my way cautiously toward the guard post. I made certain that we could not be seen from it, then I snuck back to her. Within minutes we were past and had melted into the moonlit shadows of the hill.

There are few trees in this barren land, but bushes grow sparsely here and there. We kept to them as much as possible. I cursed the moonlight for being so bright, but then, as if in answer to my curse, clouds rolled in and hid the moon. Just in time—after we crested the brow of Montjoie and started down the other side there was practically no covering at all.

It took us longer than I had thought to make our way close to the walls of Jerusalem. We were still a fair piece off when Yusra pulled me to a halt.

"You must not go any farther, Matthew," she said, so quietly I could hardly hear her. "It is almost dawn and you must be back under cover before the sun rises."

"I cannot leave you here," I answered.

"You must," she insisted.

"It would not be safe," I protested in a whisper.

"It is perfectly safe. There is no one about out here at night," she said.

"But Yusra . . ." I stammered.

"You cannot come right up to the walls with me, Matthew. You would be caught for certain. You know that. It is what we decided." Her voice was firm.

We had planned it all out. She had reassured me over and over that all she had to do was identify herself and she would be let in. She had no doubt at all that she would be taken care of.

"I will say, 'Ashadu an lailaha illallahu, Muhammadur rasullallah,'" Yusra said. "I bear witness that there is no god but God and Muhammad is his messenger—remember? That is all I need. I will tell them I escaped from your camp and they will welcome me. The Muslim women will accept me as one of their own, as if I were one of their own daughters, returned from being lost. I know this, Matthew."

It had seemed logical the night before. But now . . .

"This is—" A mistake, I almost said. This is all a mistake! I will wed you, Yusra, I almost said. I will take care of you. The words were filling my mouth, begging to burst out.

"Matthew," she said, "you have saved my life twice. Once by rescuing me from the sea and now a second time by giving me this chance to return where I belong. You have been good to me and you have helped me. I can never tell you how grateful I am to you. But I must go on from here by myself."

The black bulk of Jerusalem's walls loomed behind her. I felt her hand brush my cheek lightly.

"Assalamu alaikum," she whispered, then disappeared into the darkness.

I wanted to call after her, but knew I could not. I waited until I heard a man's challenge echo across the space between the city walls and myself. Yusra's clear voice answered. There was a clanking and thudding of bars being lifted, a brief flash of torchlight, then the gate swung shut again and there was nothing more but silence.

I turned and made my way back to the camp.

Soon after I arrived I heard the Muslim call to prayer begin. When it died away the first rays of sun began to lighten the sky.

The fourth day of July

We began our withdrawal today. I rode to the top of Montjoie with the early morning light and looked toward Jerusalem for the last time. Then I took my place beside the king.

†   †   †

The second day of September

It is over. We have spent the summer fighting fiercely for Jaffa. If that city had fallen our remaining kingdom in the Holy Land would have been cut in two, and it could never have survived. The king fought like a giant, as usual, but after our victory he fell ill. I think the heart had almost gone out of him.

But the Saracen forces too are worn out and dispirited. The country throughout the Holy Land has been ruined, trampled underfoot by battle. There is little forage for any army's horses, and we know from our scouts and spies that Salah-ud-Din's forces are beaten down and sick. Jerusalem is suffering too. All its supplies have to come from Egypt and our armies have been successful in cutting off much of that route. The caravans bearing supplies are now forced to face the murderous perils of the desert and many do not arrive. Christians and Muslims alike, we have ground each other down to despair. I have not even had the heart to write in my journal, but now I must record this ending of our great and glorious crusade.

One morning last week a Saracen band rode into Jaffa under a flag of truce. It bore word from Salah-ud-Din saying that he would negotiate. King Richard invited the sultan to come to Jaffa to talk with him. Salah-ud-Din accepted.

"I am weary, Matthew," the king said to me as we waited in his pavilion for the Turkish delegation. "It is time to make peace and go home."

I looked at him in astonishment. This was not the radiant king who had sailed so triumphantly into Messina's harbor so long ago. He put a hand on my shoulder, almost as if for support, and then stood to receive the sultan.

It was the first time I had seen Salah-ud-Din at such close quarters. He is as imposing a figure as I had imagined. Richly robed and turbaned, he strode into King Richard's tent as forcefully as the wind sweeps across the hills of Judea. He is not tall, but seems so. He is blind in one eye, but the other flashes with a brilliant intelligence.

The courtesies were observed, then all sat down. Food and drink were served. It was hours later when the two rulers began to hammer out their truce. I filled parchment after parchment.

It is to be a three-year truce. From Tyre to Jaffa the coast is to remain in Christian hands. Jerusalem is to be kept by the Muslims, but Christian pilgrims will be free to visit the city. King Richard will not do so. Neither will I.

† † †

It is late now and as I write this I am looking at the small blue bottle I rescued from the sands of Caesarea. It sits on a box in front of me, gleaming in the light of my candle. Such a fragile object to have survived for so many hundreds of years. Cities have fallen, men have died, but it endures. Will King Richard's truce endure so well, I wonder?

Most of the crusaders feel it is a defeat. I know the king does. But I do not. We have saved our kingdom in the Holy Land, even if it is much reduced. Our pilgrims will have access to the Holy City. And the bloodshed will cease. Muslims and Christians will live side by side in peace. I cannot believe this is failure.

King Richard will return to England now and I shall go with him.

With me goes the true account of this crusade. And the small blue bottle.

Acknowledgements

I would like to thank the Canada Council for the grant that enabled me to research and write this novel.

I also wish to thank Rukhsana Khan for her invaluable help and advice.